Silent Lee

and the

Oxford Adventure

Silent Lee

and the

Oxford Adventure

ALEX HIAM

Silent Lee and the Oxford Adventure

Copyright ©2020 by Alex Hiam

Webster Press, LLC

Published by
Webster Press, LLC

ISBN: 978-1-63558-014-3
eISBN: 978-1-63558-015-0

Cover and Interior Design: GKS Creative
Copyediting and Proofreading: Kim Bookless
Project Management: The Cadence Group
Story Development: Sadie Hiam

I often think back to my visits with my great-grandmother, Jane Webster, who introduced me to the side door world. She was in her eighties and nineties when I was a child, and my twin brother and I spent long hours exploring her mysterious mansion on Dartmouth Street in Boston. It was full of narrow stairs behind secret panels leading to hidden rooms. Aunt Gen is modeled on her kind personality, and Silent's school is set in a sprawling old mansion based on her Dartmouth Street house. So, a dedication to my great-grandmother. Thanks for all the magical memories!

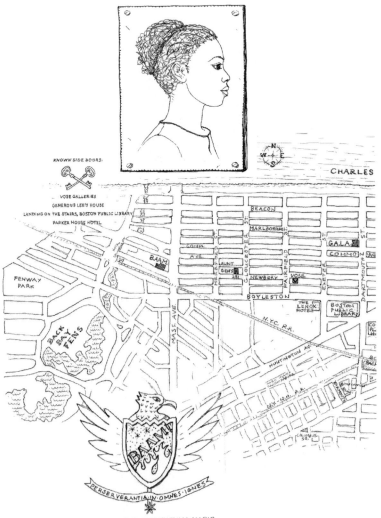

KNOWN SIDE DOORS:

VOSE GALLERIES
GENEROUS LEE'S HOUSE
LANDING ON THE STAIRS, BOSTON PUBLIC LIBRARY
PARKER HOUSE HOTEL

CHARLES

BEACON
MARLBOROUGH
G.A.L.A.
COMMON
NEWBURY
VOSE
BOYLSTON
THE LENOX HOTEL
BOSTON PUBLIC LIBRARY
N.Y.C. R.R.
HUNTINGTON AV.
N.Y. N.H. R.R.

FENWAY PARK

BACK BAY FENS

COMM. AVE
GLOUCESTER ST
AUNT GEN'S
MASS AVE
EXETER
BAAM

PERSERVERANTIA·IN·OMNES·IGNES

BOY'S ACADEMY OF ALCHEMY & MAGIC

Silent Lee's Side Door World

RIVER

PUBLIC

GARDEN

COMMON

BACK BAY
BOSTON

GIRL'S ACADEMY OF
LATIN AND ALCHEMY

A Secret Enemy

A lean, bearded man crouched by an iron fence on a sidewalk along Newbury Street on a stormy night. Beside him on the brick sidewalk, a snake coiled and uncoiled, hissing angrily in a wire cage.

It was a rainy early September night in old-fashioned Boston, and the street was empty except for the very occasional horse-drawn carriage splashing past. The man ignored the carriages and they ignored him. A magical working concentrated the shadows to make him for all practical purposes invisible. He was expert at workings, weavings, wards, and many other forms of magic. His name was Godfrey Saint-Omer, the newly appointed dueling master at the Boy's Academy of Alchemy and Magic. (The headmaster had hired him in a hurry when the previous dueling master had resigned due to work-related injuries. Teaching magical dueling was an accident-prone occupation, and the headmaster was so relieved that anyone actually wanted to do it that he had overlooked Saint-Omer's lack of references.)

The quiet was interrupted by the *putt-putt-putt* of a Model T station hack coming up the road. "Here they are," Saint-Omer muttered. "Time for *you* to go to work." He opened the cage and, reciting in ancient Egyptian, pointed toward the neat garden on the other side of the fence.

The viper slithered under the fence, the man hurried away, and the old-fashioned taxicab pulled up to the curb.

Two people got out of the taxi—an older woman named Generous Lee and her fifteen-year-old great niece, Silent. It was two o'clock in the morning, which puts us a couple hours ahead of their story. Let's go back and join them.

ONE

The Great Horned Owl

Shortly past midnight, Silent Lee and her Great Aunt Generous finally went to bed. They'd stayed up late putting the house back together after Silent's mother had packed all their belongings to send to CIA headquarters. Last summer, Sie's mother had announced that Aunt Gen was dead and had taken possession of her house with its *very* unusual side door, which serves as a portal between two adjacent worlds.

It had been a rough time for Silent—and also for Aunt Gen, who had been interrogated in a CIA safe house. Fortunately, Sie and her new friend, Raahi, had uncovered the plot, rescued her aunt, and saved the side door. Now they were back home and Sie was in her own bed for the first time in months.

But just before she fell asleep, she thought of something that made her sit up and throw off the covers. "Darn!" she exclaimed. "I left my birth certificate in the cousins' attic!" (That's where her mother had sent her to stay.)

Things had been so unsettled that Sie hadn't even had a chance to open the envelope and look at the certificate. "I shouldn't have left it there," she exclaimed. Normally she kept her thoughts to herself, but she was so annoyed that the words just popped out.

A light came on outside her bedroom.

"Is that you, Auntie?" she asked.

"Yes, dear. I heard you talking to yourself and I agree. We really should get that document. Where did you leave it?"

"On my sleeping bag in the cousins' attic. That's where my 'bedroom' was. But they're probably back from summer vacation, and they aren't exactly the friendliest."

"I'm sure we'll think of something. Come on."

Hurrying out the front door dressed in slippers and bathrobes over PJs with only a chanted moisture-repellant spell for protection from the rain, they made their way to an old-fashioned depot hack—a wooden taxicab on a Model T body—that was waiting for them. The white-whiskered driver touched his tweed cap and off they went, *putt-putting* through modern Boston with sleek cars and neon signs all around them.

The antique vehicle hiccupped to a stop on a side street and Silent helped her aunt climb down. It was a residential neighborhood and very quiet at that hour of night. Silent's friend, Raahi, lived at the other end of the block in a basement apartment with his mother, but Silent did not want to bother him in the middle of the night. Her focus was on the cousins' house.

A streetlight flickered through a maple tree, showing a bent aluminum gate opening onto a short path. The path led to cement steps and a door with flaking gray paint. It was the same familiar kitchen door that she remembered from her unpleasant stay there. A porch light was on and moths circled it, but the windows of the house were dark.

Silent frowned as she spotted the cousins' beat up minivan parked nearby. "They're home," she whispered. "How are we going to get in?"

"*We* aren't," Aunt Gen whispered back. A large owl swooped out of the night and perched on the lantern. The moths fled.

"Is that your doing?" Sie asked, an eyebrow arching in surprise.

"She's a great horned owl," Aunt Gen said. "I summoned her. Do you want to direct her?"

"I'll give it a try." Silent closed her eyes and slipped into the magical meditation state she'd been taught at school, reaching out and feeling for the consciousness of the owl. She'd connected with birds before, mostly sparrows, but was unprepared for the owl's presence. The bird was so powerful that it seemed to be probing around in *her* mind—quite the opposite of what was supposed to happen.

She decided to take a respectful approach. Making a mental bow, she said, "I'm sorry to bother you, but I was hoping you could help us with a small favor."

"What do you have for me?" the owl demanded.

"Oh, ah . . . I don't have anything right now, but—"

The owl cut the connection and spread its wings.

Aunt Gen snapped her fingers and, with a loud rustling, a squirrel tumbled out of the maple tree. Before it could get its bearings and run back to the tree, the owl was on it.

Sie looked away as strong talons and beak tore into it.

The owl satisfied its hunger then reconnected with Sie. "What?" it demanded.

"Oh! Ah, go in the top window. It's open."

"And then?" the owl asked.

"A paper in an envelope. Lying on my sleeping bag or near it."

"Show me."

Of course the owl doesn't know those words, Silent thought, so she visualized the paper, the attic, and her improvised bed.

The owl circled up to the attic window. As soon as it slid into the deeper darkness of the house, Silent turned to her aunt. "That was so unnecessary!" she hissed. "I have half a mind to reweave the entire event!"

"Your sympathies are with the squirrel?"

"Aren't yours?"

"The owl was going to eat dinner anyway," Aunt Gen said. "I just saved it the trouble of hunting."

"Why use an owl instead of just summoning the paper?"

"Do you remember *precisely* where you left it?"

"Of course I do! On my sleeping bag. Or the floor beside it. Or I might've slipped it under something." Sie frowned.

"When you don't know where something is, you can't summon it. You need to hunt for it, my dear. And hunters like fresh meat. That's why—"

"The owl's trying to reach me." Silent closed her eyes and returned to the trance. A powerful image of one of her books came to her with talons poking holes in its cover. The visual image was surprisingly clear, considering that the attic was pitch dark, but it was without color. *They see in shades of gray,* Sie thought. Then she collected her wits and sent back, "No, more like this," and formed a picture in her mind of the envelope holding the birth certificate.

The owl, keeping the connection open, scanned across the rough floorboards and onto her sleeping bag. "Wait," Sie said to it through the trance. "That's it," she added as the owl's gaze swung back to a sheet of paper laying on the bag. The owl moved closer and Sie could actually see the writing well enough to make out individual words. It was her birth certificate all right; it had her name at the top along with a date, and below it, a line with a name for her mother. The line for her father was left blank.

She was surprised that the certificate was out of its sealed envelope. Maybe a curious summer renter had been poking around in her things. "Show me again," she thought, puzzled by the image the owl had sent, but the owl's vision was swiveling away. Quickly she added, "Bring it, please. Thank you!"

The owl swooped low over them, a flapping sheet of paper clasped in its hooked talons. As it passed overhead, it let go of the paper and Sie reached out to catch it—but an unexpected gust of wind swished it out of her grasp.

"There!" Aunt Gen said. "Mission accomplished." She was holding the birth certificate. "Take us home before the rain starts again, George," she added as she climbed into the station hack, still holding the paper.

"May I have it?" Sie asked.

"Eventually, my dear. Was it in the bottom of the birdcage when you first found it?"

"Yes. You left some things for me. When, uh, when I thought you were dead."

Aunt Gen nodded. "And you brought my birdcage here with you. But I wasn't dead, was I?"

"Thankfully, no."

The car began to pull away from the curb then braked and stopped unexpectedly.

"Sorry," the driver said, "but . . ."

The headlights showed a man standing in the street in front of them. They'd nearly hit him.

He had a fedora-style felt hat and round glasses that were misted with water droplets. It was beginning to rain again. Oddly, considering the damp weather, he had a large, antique-looking book under one arm. He blinked as if the headlights had startled him.

Aunt Gen climbed out of the car and hurried up to him. "Is something wrong?" she asked.

He leaned toward her and she listened intently, but Silent could not hear what he was saying over the rattle of the idling motor and the sound of rain on the wooden roof above her head. Aunt Gen nodded and said, this time loud enough for all to hear, "Thank you for the warning. We'll be careful."

As Sie studied them, a stray thought struck her. *His complexion is darker than Auntie's,* she thought, *but he looks a little like me and if you blended them, you'd get* my *skin tone.*

Aunt Gen came back to the side of the hack and said, "Give me your hand, Silent. I'm getting too old to climb in and out of vehicles."

When Silent looked forward again, the man was gone. "Wasn't that the Custodian from the Boston Public Library?" she asked.

"That's right," Aunt Gen said. "He's a very old friend."

"Who just happens to visit you in the middle of a rainy night when you're sneaking out in your bathrobe to retrieve a mysterious document?"

"Our use of magic attracted his attention, but I like the way you ask questions," Aunt Gen said. "You're observant and inquisitive. Such good qualities!"

"And is being evasive a good quality?" Silent asked.

"Sometimes," Aunt Gen said. "George? The Custodian thinks we should not return by the same route we used to get here."

The driver touched his hat.

"Wait, did we just . . ." Sie had experienced a brief sense of dizziness, like when she stepped through the side door. Now the street was cobbled, with lanterns on posts with flickering gas jets that cast a warm halo in the rainy mist—but in many of the older neighborhoods, modern Boston still used old-fashioned gas lamps. Silent peered around, looking for other clues. *No electric lights at any of the doors,* she thought, *so definitely the side door world, but how did we—*

"George has a remarkable talent for travel," Aunt Gen said. "He really is my favorite driver. Now, where were we?"

"We *were* in the modern world retrieving my birth certificate and trying not to run over the local Custodian. Why was he warning you? About what?"

Aunt Gen nodded. "I don't think it's anything important, dear. By the way, do you recall the exact circumstances under which you found this document?"

Sie did not reply.

"When your mother told you I was dead and hid me in a safe house, I used what magic I could muster to reach out and pack a box for you to find. Which you did, thank goodness! But since the reports of my death proved to be false . . ."

"You're going to keep my birth certificate secret?" Sie finished.

Aunt Gen nodded again.

"I got a glimpse of it through the owl's eyes."

"Did you?" Aunt Gen sounded surprised.

"And I noticed that Mother's name isn't on it."

"Ah."

"The name I saw was Susan LeGreen. Actually I think it said 'Sue O. LeGreen,' which is odd in several ways."

"Is it?"

"First, 'Sue' is a nickname, so why didn't she sign it 'Susan'? And why not spell out her whole middle name? People usually use full names on legal documents."

"I see," Aunt Gen said. "Oddly casual, you're thinking?"

"Yes. And I've never even *heard* of her. Is 'LeGreen' even a family name, or was I adopted? Because I don't exactly look like my, uh, not-mother, do I?"

"No, you don't," Aunt Gen agreed. "What else?"

"My birthdate. It was a hundred years off."

"You saw all that?" Aunt Gen asked, sounding surprised.

"The date makes no sense unless I was born in the side door world, which is about a century different from modern Boston. *Was* I?"

"Excellent questions, my dear! And at some point in the future, I look forward to explaining why I had your mother step in and take on that role. But the story goes further back than that. Did you know that *she* was adopted into the family?"

"What?"

TWO

The Viper

"Wait, my mother was adopted?" Silent exclaimed. "By who? You?"

"Your mother wasn't always a CIA operative, of course. As a young child, she was adopted by a distant cousin of mine out in Chicago," Aunt Gen explained as they *putt-putted* through the quiet nighttime streets. "She came to Boston for college and I used to have her over for Sunday dinners. Her parents asked me to keep an eye on her."

"Is that why she can't do magic?" Sie asked.

"Not at all magical. I tried to teach her but had to give up. It didn't really matter, though, because she went to nonmagical schools in the modern world."

"And then? Did she use a fake name on my birth certificate, or was *I* adopted too?"

"The reason I had her act as your mother in the modern world was my age, at least partly, my dear. Ah, we're almost home," she added as the headlights illuminated turn-of-the-century Newbury Street. (Unfortunately they didn't notice the strange man carrying an empty wire cage as he slipped away down the dark sidewalk.) "I was obviously too old to be your mother," Aunt Generous continued, "and I'd also been very active in, well, I don't suppose it's such a secret after your recent adventures."

"You were a Custodian and your job was to guard against misuse of magic?" Sie guessed.

"Yes. Actually, I was on a crack team of specialists called in to help local Custodians in emergencies."

"Were you higher ranked than a Custodian, then?"

"Oh yes," Aunt Gen said. "We were interworld in scope and we received highly specialized training. There may still be crack teams operating, but since I'm retired I wouldn't know."

"Wait, is 'crack team' just an old-fashioned expression, or is it an actual term?"

Aunt Gen nodded. "Another good question, my dear. It stood for, well . . ." There was a pause.

"Come on, Auntie!"

"You can't ask *any* more questions if I tell you."

Sigh. "All right."

"Custodial Rescues And Classified—uh, well—Kills."

"What? Wait, were you some sort of magical assassin?"

"It means we had the authority to take extreme measures *only* when absolutely necessary. But I told you, no more questions."

"About CRACK teams, all right, but we were talking about me. Did you do this when I was a baby?"

"I retired around the time you were born." Aunt Gen smiled and leaned over to peck a kiss onto her cheek. "But I did not, ah, officially adopt you myself because I was worried that old enemies might try to take advantage of the situation."

"What situation?" Sie demanded.

"Loved ones can be taken hostage or threatened in order to gain leverage over operatives, so I didn't want it to appear that you were all *that* close to me. Otherwise I could have just adopted you myself, I suppose. In hindsight . . ."

"Yes, it would have been better than trusting my mother—or whoever she actually was. Some very distant cousin from Chicago. I can't *believe* . . ." Silent frowned and bit her lip. It would be natural to be angry at Aunt Gen, but having nearly lost her so recently, she didn't want to be. "At least I can say I'm glad she's not my real mom," Sie said instead. "She was so awful about the side door, and she never seemed to take much interest in me even when I was little. I haven't heard from her at all. Have you?"

"No, but I heard a rumor that she's been demoted and sent to work in Argentina. I have no idea why, but of course she never told us anything about her work, even before she turned against us."

"I wonder if she'll send a box full of some weird South American spices next Christmas. But who is the woman on my birth certificate, Susan LeGreen? *Another* distant cousin?"

"I'm sorry not to have been completely honest with you."

"*Are* you?" Silent asked, eyeing her.

"Am I sorry? Of course! You can let us out here, George. Thank you."

"No, are you being 'completely honest' even now?" Sie asked as they got out. "Because you're ducking most of my questions. When can I meet her?"

"I'm being as honest as I feel I can be, my dear. Do you have your key?"

"If we go in the front door, will the younger you be at home? I could ask her."

"If I'm not out on some mission," Aunt Gen said. "But we don't live then. We live in modern Boston, which right now is through the side door, and it must be nearly two o'clock in the morning. Let's get to bed."

Silent reached for the key on its string around her neck and held it up. "All right," she said, "but we're not done talking about my birth certificate."

"I'm sorry, dear, but actually, we are."

Sie felt annoyed as they let themselves in through the little side gate and walked along the snaking garden path beside the dark house, but she couldn't think of what to say that might change her aunt's mind.

"I should've brought a lantern," Aunt Gen said, pausing. "I seem to have gotten my bathrobe tangled in a rosebush. Can you free it?"

"Maybe we shouldn't have gone out in bathrobes. Wait, don't pull. I'll . . ." Silent leaned over, trying to see, but it was too dark. Considering how thorny her aunt's rosebushes were, she was hesitant to deal with the problem by feel alone, and Aunt Gen did *not* approve of highly visible public displays of magic such as weaving a ball of light to see in the dark.

"I wish I could see like an owl," Sie said.

"You can," Aunt Gen replied. "Just summon that owl again. I think she still owes us a favor. That was a nice, plump squirrel we gave her."

"Really, Auntie! You know how I feel about that. Besides, the owl was in the modern world, which we left when we were driving."

"That doesn't matter to an owl," Aunt Gen said. "They slip between worlds with ease. You'd be surprised how big a hunting territory an owl can have. There, I've made the link again. See if you can sense her."

Pop. Swish. A large owl appeared over their heads and circled around them.

"Oh!" Sie exclaimed. "Well, all right. Here goes," she added as she entered the connecting trance.

"What now?" the owl demanded—so strongly that Silent winced.

"Can I please see through your eyes again? I want to see—"

"The snake?" the owl finished, swooping over again.

And as it flew by, Sie got a strong, clear image of the garden around their feet. Instead of the thorn she imagined was hooked on Aunt Gen's bathrobe, there was a horned snake biting a corner of the fabric. "Don't move!" she exclaimed. "It's a snake!"

"Goodness me, let's not be dramatic," Aunt Gen said. "There aren't poisonous snakes in downtown Boston, my dear." She was about to reach down to try to free it, but Silent grabbed her wrist.

The owl veered off and landed on the iron railing of the garden fence, from where it sent a puzzled question about the snake. But Sie ignored the owl and focused on her breathing, which was shallow and fast. She was in a panic, her heart racing, and she knew she couldn't control magic while panicked. Calming herself firmly, she took a deep, steady breath and let it out, breathing it toward the snake.

"Careful!" Aunt Gen cried as a jet of flame burst brightly toward the hem of her bathrobe. Silent had used her breath to direct a fire-weaving—a very difficult-to-control piece of magic that they had covered in a lecture last spring at GALA—the Girl's Academy of Latin and Alchemy, where Sie had been at school until her mother faked her aunt's death. But students were not allowed to practice fire-weavings for fear of burning the school down, so Sie had experimented when no one was watching. It's true that she'd accidentally lit a trash can on fire and had to summon rain, but now she was pleased she'd practiced.

The snake let go, slithering rapidly to the side as flame reached toward it.

Aunt Gen spoke something in what Sie thought was ancient Egyptian, but she wasn't sure because they didn't study that particular magic in school; it was considered far too dangerous. (Sie made a mental note to look up Egyptian transport spells in Aunt Gen's library.) "I sent it back," Aunt Gen said. "It belongs in the North African desert, not here. And next time, can you please use something less flashy?"

"Your robe's on fire," Silent said. "Want me to . . ."

"I'll take care of it," Aunt Gen said, waving a hand in the air and putting the fire out. "Another gift for the owl would be polite. She probably expected to eat the snake."

With a wave of her hand, Aunt Gen produced yet another falling squirrel, but Sie was ready this time and rolled it under a thick rosebush with a puff of wind. Then, with a *pop*, she summoned a chicken drumstick from their kitchen. It had been in a bowl of leftovers from dinner.

The owl spread its wings and swooped silently down to the garden path, where it landed and examined the chicken leg. "It's from a bird," Sie said, pushing the image of a chicken into the owl's mind. "Cooked," she added, visualizing fire beneath it.

The owl pecked at it, then, seemingly satisfied, grasped it in a talon and ghosted off into the night. Silent thought she heard a faint *pop* as it passed over the front gate and disappeared. *Back to the modern world*, Sie thought. *Or maybe another world we don't even know about.* She turned back to Aunt Gen. "Why was there an Egyptian snake in our garden?"

Aun Gen frowned. "I think the more relevant question is, why *that* one? Do you have your key ready?"

"That one? What do you mean?"

"The Egyptian horned viper. Why choose that snake if you want to kill someone? It's poisonous, for sure, but rarely deadly, at least if you seek treatment right away."

"It *could* have killed you," Sie said. "And someone must've sent it here. Who?"

Aunt Gen paused on the landing outside the side door. "Yes, but you see, if you're going to bother to bring a snake all the way from Egypt to kill someone, the obvious choice is the Egyptian hooded cobra. Their venom is fast acting and extremely deadly. That's what did in Queen Cleopatra."

"Auntie, you're overanalyzing. Maybe it was the first poisonous snake they were able to find."

"And maybe it just escaped from the zoo. But *I* think someone was testing us to see how we'd handle it. The question is, why?"

"Or who," Sie said with a frown.

"Who's testing us, or which of us is being tested?" Aunt Gen asked.

"I don't care. I'm exhausted."

And then they stepped inside and locked the door behind them.

As Sie stumbled back to bed, her mind was full of questions and suspicions. But tomorrow was the first day of ninth grade at the Girl's Academy of Latin and Alchemy, and she really wanted to get some sleep before the sun rose.

She tossed and turned as images of owls, vipers, and birth certificates whirled in her mind until she heard a snake tell her that her real mother was Queen Cleopatra and she realized she must be dreaming.

THREE

Advanced Alchemy

The side-door version of Boston was bustling with horse-drawn carriages and the occasional motorcar as Silent walked to school. Even though she'd gotten only a few hours of sleep, she made it there in good time and found her friend Ali waiting on the sidewalk.

There was a lot to talk about—she had not seen Ali since Great Aunt Gen's rescue—but they had to confine themselves to secretive whispers as they hurried through the tall iron gates of the Girl's Academy of Latin and Alchemy, GALA for short.

Everyone crowded into the first-day-of-school assembly, where the headmistress spoke about safety, safety, and more safety. GALA being a school for the study of magic, there were a *great* many things that could go wrong. The headmistress had a bad habit of retelling many of the worst stories of magical accidents: the place-loop accidentally set on the front door that spat you back into the school when you tried to leave at the end of the day; a whirlwind woven by a student for a prank that accidentally mixed several explosive alchemical ingredients; and a group of seniors who used a forbidden transport spell to sneak off campus during lunch, only to find upon transporting back that they'd recombined their body parts so that one of them had another's head, hands were mixed up, and so forth—that accident took a *long* time to put right. But Sie and Ali had heard most of the stories before and were unimpressed.

After assembly, the students—in their uniform gray skirts, dark gray stockings, white blouses, and blue blazers—hurried off to their classes.

Sie and Ali went in different directions. Sie's first class was an advanced alchemy lab.

The alchemy labs were held in a long, marble-floored room with windows on one side, a blackboard down the other, and a central workbench with stools. The instructor stood near the door. The students joked that she wanted to be the first to leave if an experiment went wrong, but it may have been true. Silent was in the top-level lab class with a dozen other advanced students, most of them seniors and several years older than her. (GALA went all the way through high school.) Things tended to explode when Ali did lab work, so she had been assigned to a lower-level lecture instead.

Sie found herself between The Twins—Ruby on her left, long blonde hair swishing over the burners as she leaned in front of Sie to talk to her sister, Lula. Similarly, Lula's long blonde hair seemed to want to ignite itself whenever she leaned over to whisper to Ruby. Sie muttered a fire suppression chant when she noticed a strand of hair beginning to smoke.

Sie was a natural at most forms of magic but not as gifted at alchemy as The Twins. "It's all very well if *you* don't want to listen," she muttered to them, "but I can't hear when you're talking!"

"Miss Lee! Do you have something you wish to contribute?" It was Master Medera, a thin, tight-lipped woman with white hair pulled back in a very firm bun.

"I'm sorry," Sie said. "I didn't think you'd hear me." And of course, as soon as she said this, she regretted it.

The master put down her chalk and walked along the workbench until she was standing behind Sie. "What, precisely, is it that you don't want me to hear?" she hissed.

"I didn't mean it that way," Sie hurried to explain, trying to look over her shoulder but unable to turn enough to see Master Medera clearly. (She thought of the owl; it would have been able to turn its head and meet the teacher's gaze.) "Sorry." If she complained about The Twins, they would probably sabotage her work.

"Were you asking them for help?" Master Medera leaned over the bench, taking in Sie's careful progress (she had been following each step and taking time to measure accurately) compared to the startling progress of The Twins. "Isn't this remarkable?" Master Medera added, sounding quite pleased. "Ruby and Lula have already completed today's lab! Very nice work, girls, but don't help Silent. She ought to do it for herself. Now," she added as she walked back to the front of the room, "who can tell me what this sequence is intended to produce?"

Silent's hand went up. Based on the equations on the board, the product of their experiment was supposed to be a sweet elixir that contained a small amount of Sa'āda, or human happiness, according to the *Kimiya-yi Sa'ādat*, an ancient alchemical text.

Master Medera frowned and waited for another hand to go up. Finally an eleventh grader offered an answer. "That's correct," Master Medera said. "Now get back to work! I want your results by end of class. You'll test them on each other before you leave."

On each other? Sie glanced at The Twins, who were whispering again and seemed very amused. *I hope I don't have to try theirs!*

She finished her work before the bell and looked up as the instructor cleared her throat. "Turn off your burners and speak a cooling charm. Now, each of you turn to your neighbor and offer them a teaspoon of your elixir. That should be enough to keep you in a good mood for the rest of the day."

By the time Sie had put away her lab equipment and packed up her notes, she was crying. Tears insisted on raining down her cheeks and she could barely stifle sobs as she went to meet Ali in the lounge. She had already soaked her handkerchief (all the girls carried them; disposable tissues hadn't been invented in the side door world).

"What's the matter?" Ali looked alarmed. "Did something bad happen?"

Sie, who under normal circumstances never cried, had to wipe her face on her sleeve. "No,"—*sob*—"The Twins did something to their"—*sob*—"elixir to give it an opposite effect!"

"It was supposed to make you happy?"

Sie nodded and sniffed.

"We should report them!"

"On the first day?" Sie exclaimed, wiping with the other sleeve. "I don't want to start out on the wrong foot. It's going to be—*sniff*—a terrible year!—*sniff, sniff*—Do you think you can take this off me?"

"An alchemical reaction? No way. Did you finish *your* elixir?"

Sie nodded, bleary eyed, and sat down with a thump.

"Get up. Quick." Ali tugged her to her feet. "Before the next lab starts!" And then she was hurrying Sie out of the lounge, down the stairs to the basement, and, with a brief stop to hide in a broom closet while a group of masters walked past, into the lab itself. The door was ajar and no one was there. "Where's yours? You always do them right."

Sie began to sob quietly into her soaking wet handkerchief. "There's no use!—*sniff, sniff*—I'm going to flunk out."

"Get a hold of yourself," Ali hissed. "Someone's going to hear us." She hurried to the far end of the lab and tried to turn the brass handles on the tall storage cabinet. "Locked," she announced. "Come here. I'm not as good as you at openings."

Sie did not respond.

"Oh well, here goes," Ali said. "*Vi aperta armarium!*" she commanded, her hands held up, palms toward the cupboard.

Sie stopped blowing her nose and turned to see. At first, nothing, then the sound of glass breaking.

Ali frowned and tried the handles. "Still locked," she complained. "Maybe you should try."

There were cracks and snaps and shattering sounds, louder and louder, as if everything inside the cupboard was breaking at once. "Darn it!" Ali exclaimed, backing up. "That's not supposed to—"

"*Mane! Morari! Restituere integritatem, statim!*" It was Sie, rushing toward Ali and the cabinet.

The sounds stopped.

They looked at each other.

Sie reached out and, with a muttered "*Reserare,*" tried the handles.

The doors swung slowly open. The shelves were all in neat order, jars and beakers and retorts and the little drawers with their little labels for ingredients, just as they ought to be. And there, in the middle of a shelf along with the rest of her class's work, was a vial labeled "Silent Lee, Experiment #1." Ali reached for it, but Sie said, "Let me."

"Drink it all," Ali said. "And hurry! I think I hear footsteps in the hall."

Sie was back to as-normal-as-usual by the time school ended and they walked through the tiled hall and out the wrought iron gate of the Girl's Academy of Latin and Alchemy into the warm, golden afternoon. The haze had burned off and it felt like it was still high summer.

They had paused on the sidewalk to talk about their day when a shiny black carriage raced past them, pulled by a pair of shiny black horses. The coachman sat stiffly in a black tailcoat, and his whip, which snapped loudly, was made of black leather. Traffic was light, but even so, the haste of the driver caused trouble, forcing a rider and another carriage to swerve out of the way.

It might have been—most likely was—just a coincidence that a limb fell from one of the old trees lining the sidewalk. The *crack* of it breaking made Sie look up just in time to mutter a weaving that pushed it to the side with a puff of strong wind.

It gave Ali quite a start when it thumped down beside them. She shrieked.

"Calm down," Sie said. "It didn't hit us."

"The carriage or the branch?" Ali demanded, looking upset.

"Neither."

"Easy for *you* to be calm," Ali complained. "You're full of that elixir!"

"I'm in a better mood, it's true," Sie admitted. "Maybe it won't be such a bad year, after all. I mean, what *else* could possibly go wrong?"

"Hopefully nothing." Ali eyed her narrowly. "Is there any *other* reason you're in a good mood?"

"What are you talking about?" Sie demanded.

"*You* know," Ali teased. "Are you meeting *him*?"

"Who?" Silent asked, trying to look innocent. The topic was slightly embarrassing, at least the way Ali approached it.

"The boy you met on summer vacation, of course! Your new—"

"He's *not* my boyfriend," Sie cut in. They'd already discussed Raahi over lunch and she wasn't going to let Ali start up all over again.

"Whatever you say," Ali said. "Is he handsome?"

"He's nearly blind."

"You already told me that, but you didn't tell me what he *looks* like," Ali complained.

"Are you always this annoying?" Sie asked.

"Always," Ali said with a grin. "So, *is* he good looking?"

"I don't know. What do *you* think, Raahi?" Sie asked, turning to address a tall, dark-haired boy in thick-lensed glasses who had just come up to them on the sidewalk. He was wearing the uniform of the Boy's Academy of Alchemy and Magic: gray slacks, white Oxford shirt, finely striped red and orange tie, and a blue blazer with the school's shield embroidered on it.

The shield was encompassed by the fierce head and strong wings of an eagle; on the shield itself, block letters spelled out the school's acronym, "BAAM," over red flames. A banner below the shield held the school's motto: *"Perseverantia in omnibus ignes."* In English, "Carry on in spite of explosions."

"Very handsome," Raahi said, one corner of his mouth curling up in spite of his effort to keep a straight face.

Ali's complexion was light enough that she blushed pinkly when embarrassed, which embarrassed her even more. At this juncture, she looked more red in the face than Sie had ever seen her, which made Sie chuckle and made Ali even more embarrassed.

"This is Ali," Sie said, grinning.

"Uh, p-pleased to meet you," Ali stuttered.

"Charmed!" Raahi said, one eyebrow raised. "You've heard a lot about me."

"The expression," Sie corrected, "is '*I've* heard a lot about *you.*'"

"But I haven't," Raahi said. "Silent doesn't talk much," he explained to Ali. "She certainly doesn't gossip. Not to me at least. But I gather girls often talk among themselves?"

"That's a stereotype," Sie said. "It's so nice out, I think we should walk up to the Public Garden together. Come on." (There was a large pond where the swan boats took people on trips there, and it was on Ali's way home.)

"So, tell me about yourself, Ali," Raahi said as they headed up the sidewalk. "What kinds of magic are *you* good at?"

Ali looked stricken.

"I don't think she expected you to actually talk to her," Sie said.

"Charms?" Raahi guessed, probably just to make her blush again.

"N-no," Ali stammered.

"Her magic is strong," Silent said. "Powerful. Potent."

Raahi raised an eyebrow. "I see. Do things blow up? I hear we get a lot of that at BAAM, and even though we only had a half day today, there *was* a loud explosion."

"You better tell us all about it," Sie said. "To give Ali time to recover."

"I, uh . . ." Ali still seemed at a loss.

"I'm just teasing," Sie said. "But what blew up?"

"A lab," Raahi said. "With lots of smoke. They ran out, coughing and choking. It was quite exciting. And there was a rumor of sabotage."

"Sabotage?" Sie's eyebrows rose. "By who?"

Raahi shrugged. "I didn't see much." He looked closely at Ali to see if she got it, which made her blush again. (Raahi was functionally blind due to tunnel vision, meaning he had clear vision only in a narrow cone directly ahead, but that and a bright light were enough for him to devour books, which was his favorite thing to do aside from going on magical adventures.) "I heard," Raahi continued, "that some of the boys saw a mysterious black carriage pulled by black horses racing away just after the explosion."

"That's circumstantial," Sie said, "but suggestive. Especially since one raced by *us* just as we got out of school."

"Coincidences are for magidiots," Ali said, quoting an impolite but widespread proverb (the idea being that people without magic often think magical events happen just by chance, but of course they don't).

"Oh, she speaks!" Raahi smiled. "Did anything blow up at *your* school today?"

"N-no . . . but someone sabotaged Sie's elixir!" Ali said, excitement overcoming her shyness.

"It's true," Sie said. "But Ali saved me. Want to go for a ride on a swan boat?" she added as they entered the park.

"I should really be getting home," Ali said.

"Too bad," Raahi said, "since you only just found your voice."

At that, Ali blushed again and rushed off.

"I think you made an impression on her," Sie said.

"She seems nice," Raahi said. "But very shy."

"Ye-es. That must be it." Sie's expression was probably too subtle for Raahi to see. "Let's cross again and head down Newbury Street."

Six busy blocks later, they reached Great Aunt Generous's house and let themselves in the gate, but of course they didn't go up to the front door. Instead, they walked along the garden path that led to the side door. Halfway there, Sie paused and pointed at sooty stains on the stone path. "I had to torch an Egyptian horned viper last night," she said, her tone matter of fact.

"What?" Raahi exclaimed, startled.

"Long story, but we went out to get something from my cousins'—on your block, actually—and on the way back, a snake nearly bit my aunt."

"An *Egyptian* snake?"

Sie shrugged. "Maybe someone keeps exotic pets and one got away."

"Maybe." But Raahi frowned.

At the top of the narrow stairs, Sie pulled out her key and opened the door. As they stepped through, the light flickered. There was a tingling sensation, and then they were in a comfortable sitting room that looked like it belonged to the old-fashioned world they had just left. However, through the front door came faint sounds of horns honking and engines revving in rush hour traffic. "Welcome back," Sie said.

"Thanks," Raahi said, "but I'm thinking I prefer the side door world. I explored it all afternoon. It's really amazing!"

Great Aunt Generous came toward them from the back of the house, carrying a silver tray with homemade cookies and two tall glasses of milk. "How was your first day of school, Raahi?" she asked.

"Different," Raahi said. He had, through eighth grade, attended modern schools. But because he was so helpful in that summer's magical quest to save the side door, Aunt Gen had arranged for him to attend the Boy's Academy of Alchemy and Magic.

"He was just telling me about today's explosion," Sie said.

"Oh dear!" Aunt Gen's eyebrow arched. "Was anybody hurt?"

"I don't think so," Raahi said.

"Do be careful," Aunt Gen warned. "Although, fortunately, emergency medicine is more advanced in the side door world."

"Do they use magic for that?" Raahi asked.

Aunt Gen smiled. "Of course! Do you have time for a snack before you head home?"

"Maa works until six," he said, "so I'm sure she won't mind. Those cookies smell delicious!" (Raahi and his mother favored the customary Hindi spelling "Maa" instead of "Ma," although they pronounced it the same way.)

"Good. Sit down and tell me about your days. Silent, did anything blow up at GALA?"

"Not yet," Sie said, "but advanced alchemy was more challenging than I'd expected."

FOUR

The Bronze Wizard

The next morning dawned with heavy clouds, wind, and rain. *Like Auntie always says,* Sie thought, *the only certain thing about Boston weather is that it's going to change. Again.*

The knocker sounded on the front door just as Silent was getting her raincoat out of the closet. "I've got it!" she called to Aunt Gen.

Raahi hurried in, folding his dripping umbrella. "Is it raining in the side door world too?" he asked.

"I haven't checked yet," Sie said, "but probably. Close parallels have similar weather."

"Close parallels?" Raahi repeated, puzzled.

"That side door world is similar to ours," Sie said. "More so than most worlds, anyway."

"Have you been to any *other* worlds?" Raahi asked as he followed her down the front hall and into the sitting room.

"No, but they talk about them at my school. I'm sure they'll cover them at BAAM too."

"I hope so." He frowned. "I'm not used to being the worst student," he added, sounding worried.

"Worst? I doubt that," Sie said.

"It doesn't matter that I know trigonometry and calculus and I've read more history than anyone I've ever met. The history's not the same and I don't think they use the same math either."

"Actually, no. We study alchemical equations and—" She paused. Raahi was looking unhappy. "But you read my old textbooks over the summer, right?"

"You only gave me the ones about magic. I didn't realize history, math, and science were different too."

"Look, it'll just take a little while to catch up. And then . . ."

"Then you will be a rising star," Aunt Gen said as she came out of the kitchen, drying her hands on a dishcloth. "Don't worry!"

"I don't know," Raahi said. "My classmates are so good at magic that they use it to do tricks on each other." He looked a little uncomfortable as he said this.

"Did anyone do tricks on *you*?" Sie asked, frowning.

Raahi shrugged. "You can't blame them, I suppose."

"What did they do?" Sie persisted.

"Oh, um, when I unpacked my bag to do my homework . . ." He paused, looking embarrassed.

"What was in it?" Sie asked.

"Not my homework," Raahi said. "They turned it into beetles. *Lots* of beetles. Maa wasn't very happy. It took us half the night to round them up."

"Oh dear," Aunt Gen said. "It sounds like you need a ward of some kind. I think I have just the thing." She hurried out of the room and came back a minute later. "Here, slip this into your bag."

It was a smooth black stone that felt warm to the touch—except for a stripe of silver, which felt very cold.

"It's an interruption stone," Aunt Gen explained. "A layer of silver cuts it in half. When the stone senses malevolent magic, it cuts that too. It should rebound most student-level curses. Now, off you go, dears, you don't want to be late. And remember, please don't mention our side door," she added as they stepped through it.

Raahi paused at the garden gate. "Why can't I mention the side door?" he asked Sie.

"Because," Sie said, "there aren't very many of us."

"Us?"

"I'm the only person at GALA who commutes to school from another world. Side doors are rare."

"Even in the magical world?"

Sie nodded. "And most people can't go between worlds frequently. It makes them ill."

"Ill?" Raahi looked alarmed.

"Unless your internal magic is really strong. Yours is—don't worry. Auntie can always tell."

"I remember seeing the term 'betweeners' in one of the textbooks you lent me," Raahi said, "and I read that they don't have alternate selves in other worlds. That's why they're so magical. Their magic is concentrated in just one version of themselves. It also means they won't run into another version of themselves when they go to another world."

"That's true, but it's not the reason we keep side doors secret. It's because of creeps like, well, my so-called mother, who try to find doors between worlds and exploit them. So don't talk about the door unless you're *sure* you can trust someone. Like Ali. She literally can't give the secret away."

"Why not?"

"Aunt Gen put a compulsion on her when we were in second grade. That's when she came to GALA and we became friends."

"A compulsion? Wait, that's a joke, right? Magical humor?"

"No."

"Gosh. Is that even ethical?"

Sie shrugged. "After we got a little older, I told her about it. The compulsion. She already knew about the door."

"Was she angry?"

"At first. Then she got to thinking. See, it's actually really hard to keep a secret. Aunt Gen put a compulsion on *me* in my first year at GALA. She didn't take it off me until the end of third grade."

"But Ali *still* can't talk about the door?"

"The compulsion keeps her from telling anyone who doesn't already know."

"That's quite a spell."

"A compulsion is a kind of working. Don't use 'spell' all the time when you talk about magic. It's from the front door world. Most of our magic isn't done with spells. Workings, weavings, wards, and alchemy. Non-magical people call them spells, but it's not very accurate."

"Oh," Raahi said. He was remembering that he'd used the word frequently on his first day of school.

"Okay, we're going different directions here," Sie said.

"BAAM has a full day today, so I'll meet you at the house tonight," Raahi said. "I won't have time to walk by GALA."

"Right. Good luck!" She reached out and gave his hand a squeeze before he turned and strode with surprising confidence down Newbury Street. (Raahi owned a white walking stick with a red tip but did not like to use it, saying that he preferred to rely on what vision he had along with his other senses, which were highly developed to compensate.) When she looked back at the end of the block, he was gone. "I hope it goes better for you today," she muttered.

She walked to her next turn at Commonwealth Avenue, which had a long island of green dividing the road in half. A path wound through the grassy median past park benches and statues. She crossed halfway and followed the center path. The carriages on the road wouldn't splash her there like they did on the cobbled sidewalks.

She was almost to Dartmouth when she spotted a black carriage hurrying down Commonwealth Ave., its team of black horses shaking water from their manes as they stormed past.

It happened again: a loud *crack* and a large limb falling from an oak tree. And there was another sound that was almost obscured by the breaking limb: a grinding of tortured metal. At the same time as the limb fell toward her, a large bronze statue of a wizard astride a winged horse was popping the bolts that held it to its stone base—and tipping toward her!

She waved an arm and spun the thick oak branch into place to brace the statue at the same time she brought a strong wind toward it. Someone shouted "Hey!" as the wind blew their umbrella out into the street, but the statue began to tip back up until, with one final puff of wind, she had it on its base again.

People were staring, mouths open. Sie was not used to attracting so much attention. "I'm fine!" she said.

"Young woman, are you *sure* you're all right?" an elderly gentleman asked.

"Nothing broken," she said, trying to smile. But she had to admit to herself that she was a bit freaked out.

"Then you had best be going," the gentleman said, "before your enemies try again."

"It was probably just an accident," she replied as she hurried on her way. But for the rest of the walk, she glanced around suspiciously and continued to think how odd it really was. Statues don't usually fall over, any more than Egyptian snakes get loose on Newbury Street. And how often do branches fall on you? Maybe she *did* have a new enemy.

Still, nothing else happened to give her concern, except that it began to rain harder.

As she was turning onto Dartmouth Street, Ali caught up. "Hi there!" she said. "Can I share your raincoat? I forgot mine." And indeed, Ali's school blazer was getting quite wet, so Sie slipped her arms out of her raincoat sleeves and they used it as a cloak.

"Did anything strange happen to you on the way here?" she asked Ali.

"Of course not," Ali said. "So, that boy, Raahi. He uses your side door, right?" she asked, eyeing Silent.

"He has to," Sie said, "to get to this world. Did any branches fall while you were walking?"

"No, but it's stormy so I guess they might. Has he been to your house?" Ali persisted.

"Like I said, he has to use my door or he couldn't attend BAAM."

"And he's *really* not your boyfriend?" Ali demanded, eyeing her.

Sie didn't bother answering that one.

"Then why haven't *I* seen your house?" Ali asked. "After all these years! And you've been to mine lots of times."

"You know why."

"Not really," Ali said. "If you can invite *him*, why not *me*? Is it because I'm . . ."

"Ali! Of course not! You're just saying that to try to pressure me."

"Well?" Ali eyed her expectantly.

They'd reached the front of the school and other students were hurrying through the big iron gates. "All right," Sie said. "Why not?"

"You're actually inviting me?" Ali exclaimed. "I can't wait! My parents are out tonight, so it's great timing. Is your aunt a good cook? I bet she is!"

"Tonight?" Sie was startled. "Well, tea, not dinner. I haven't had a chance to talk to Aunt Gen about it, so let's not make it anything major."

"Don't worry; she loves me!" Ali said. And it was true that when they were younger and Aunt Gen used to walk Silent to school, she would often stop to talk with Ali. But that was years ago, and Silent wasn't certain how her aunt would react. Frowning, she let Ali lead the way through the crowded entry hall.

Their first subject of the morning was a lecture and they hurried toward the classroom, eager to be early enough to pick good seats. For this class, they'd learned yesterday, that meant as *far* from the front as possible.

Ironically—since they'd just been discussing the secrecy of Aunt Gen's side door—the class was called Parallel Worlds, Theory and Practice. It was taught by Master Dorsenhaal, and it focused on the ways in and out of worlds, which explained why he'd been nicknamed "Old Doors-and-Holes" by his students. But yesterday's lecture had been brutally boring. Sie was amazed that anyone could make such an interesting topic so dull.

Master Dorsenhaal spoke in a vaguely British accent, although no one seemed to know exactly where he was from. He sat very still, his white hair fanned out like some mad halo and his blue eyes blinking rapidly behind the tinted lenses of his gold-rimmed glasses (the kind that hook behind your ears so they won't fall off if you move rapidly—something he definitely did *not* do).

Perhaps, Sie thought, *when he's not teaching, he's leaping between worlds and needs to not lose his specs.* Unlike Ali, Sie was inclined to cut Master Dorsenhaal some slack because she was pretty sure she'd seen him reaching up to finger something beneath his shirt collar. His gesture reminded her of the old-fashioned key she wore on a string around her own neck, tucked carefully out of sight. But if he *did* have a key to a side door of his own, he didn't mention it. Instead, he reviewed, at yawn-inducing length, fictional ways in and out of worlds from popular literature—almost as if he were *trying* to avoid discussing real doors.

As the morning's lecture began and Master Dorsenhaal started to read in a monotone from his notes, Sie closed her eyes. It seemed like only a minute had passed when Ali shook her and hissed, "Wake up. Class is over!"

FIVE

Tea Time Tension

They'd suffered through a History of Sorcery lecture and rather enjoyed their Workings and Weavings Practicum. School lunch proved interestingly odd—the cook, having been on a world tour over the summer, decided that each dish would come from a different continent. "How many continents are there?" Ali asked.

"Seven, I think," Sie said as she studied the trays of food and tried to decide which looked the least bad.

"Then why are there thirteen options?" Ali asked, but no one seemed to have an answer.

After lunch, they broke into small groups to practice magical first aid, like they did at the beginning of every semester. Then the bell rang to signal that school was over for the day.

Silent and Ali walked down the side door world's Newbury Street together, talking and laughing. The rain had stopped and it was a lovely, warm afternoon. People were out doing their shopping or pushing baby strollers.

When they reached Aunt Gen's house, Sie led Ali along the path to the side entry, where she reached for her key and opened the door. The light flickered and she tugged Ali in, swinging the door closed and locking it from the inside.

Ali frowned as she looked around the sitting room; she'd been expecting it to look strange and modern.

"Auntie still likes to decorate like they do in your world," Sie explained.

In the distance, someone called, "Is that you, Silent? How was school today?"

"Fine!" Sie called back.

"I'm working on something," Aunt Gen said. "I'll be a few minutes. I thought we'd have a proper tea when Raahi gets here."

"About tea," Sie called. "Would it be all right if—"

"Can't hear you!" came Aunt Gen's voice, fainter.

"She must be going up to the attic," Sie said.

"How do you get to the other world?" Ali asked.

"We're already there. Come on. I'll show you." Sie went to the front door and opened it.

The door swung out onto another mild September afternoon, except in this one there were loud street sounds: honking horns, squealing truck brakes, the laughter of people thronging the sidewalks, and, overhead, the droning of a jet's engines as it gained altitude taking off from Logan Airport. Ali recoiled, a startled look on her face.

"We could get a shake. Do you know what that is?"

"It's so loud!"

"It's not as bad as it seems at first. Well, not quite as bad. It *is* crowded and noisy and less friendly, but it's safe—enough," Sie added with a frown as she thought about her misadventures over the summer. "Come on."

She led Ali, who gripped her arm tightly, down the front steps and out onto the sidewalk. They went a block north toward downtown. Ali, her mouth wide open and her eyes even wider, kept staring around in disbelief.

Feeling sorry for Ali as she jumped at a delivery truck's horn (it had been cut off by a taxi), Sie turned around and took her back toward the house. People who had just gotten out of work were hurrying toward their favorite cafes and bars, and Sie and Ali had to weave through the crowd to reach Aunt Gen's front gate.

"They're not proper houses," Ali complained as they slipped through the black iron gate and Sie swung it closed behind them.

"What do you mean?" Sie asked. She took great pride in her house and loved living on Newbury Street.

Ali paused to look up at Aunt Gen's stone and brick row house. "Your house looks nice," she said, "but what happened to the others?" She gestured down the street, where the buildings had signs advertising the stores, offices, and restaurants within them.

"It used to be families," Sie said, "but it got too expensive, so businesses moved in. There's apartments on the upper floors, though," she added hopefully.

"I'm going to pay more attention in Parallel Worlds class," Ali said, shaking her head in wonder. "I didn't really get it until now."

A white cargo van slammed on its brakes a moment too late and smashed into the bumper of a red car.

"Come back inside," Sie said. "I need to see if Raahi's here. And this takes getting used to," she added with a glance at the street, where the drivers had gotten out of their vehicles to shout at each other. Sie hurried to close the front door.

"I can't believe, well, I mean, obviously you *do* live here, but . . ." Ali shook her head again.

"We don't go out the front door that much. Auntie prefers to do her shopping in your world. Her favorite fruit market, baker, and butcher all closed years ago in this world, and she doesn't like the, uh, 'incivility,' that's what she—"

"That is *precisely* what I call it." Aunt Gen was coming down the stairs, a hand gripping the banister. She wore an elegant, old-fashioned silk gown, pale blue with embroidered chrysanthemums on it. She did not look like she lived in the modern world.

Ali smiled and, with a curtsy, said, "Pleased to see you, Miss Lee. I'm Silent's friend Altheia. Do you remember me?"

Aunt Gen came down the last few steps and stopped in front of them. "Of course! Welcome to our home, dear." She turned toward Sie. "It's nice to see her again but rather surprising to see her *here*."

"I'm sorry, Auntie. I should have checked with you first. Can she stay for tea?"

Aunt Gen swept past them into the parlor, eyeing the side door with a frown as she settled herself in a rocking chair. "Why don't you put the kettle on and prepare tea for four, Silent. I'll speak with Altheia while you're in the kitchen."

"I'm sorry if I've caused any trouble," Ali said.

"Not at all! It's just that I'd like to speak with you."

Sie exchanged a look with Ali as she headed toward the kitchen.

"Well, now, it *is* nice to see you," Aunt Gen said, turning her attention to the short, dimpled girl with wavy brown hair and light green eyes who was sitting on the edge of a couch, fiddling with the strap of her book bag.

"Are you mad that I came?" Ali asked.

Aunt Gen smiled. "No, I just want to make sure you know not to bring things between worlds. For instance . . ." She reached over and picked up a tiny black box. When she pushed a button on top of it, music burst out. "It's a modern radio. Silent got it for my birthday. Amazing, isn't it?" She turned it off and set it down again. "So small. So plastic. So out of place in your world. We don't have many modern things. Easier that way."

"Wow," Ali said, picking up the radio. "Everyone would love it! Our radios are as big as bread boxes and don't sound nearly as good."

"Yes, but it's a reveal," Aunt Gen said. "Do you know what that is?"

Ali shook her head.

"Someone might be able to deduce the existence of this world from it."

"If you don't mind my saying so, Miss Lee, we *study* parallel worlds. They're hardly a secret," Ali pointed out, putting the radio back down.

"But some people exploit other worlds. What if they saw you with this radio and followed you to find out where you'd gotten it? They might see you use the side door and try to steal the key."

"That's terrible!" Ali said. "Has anything like that actually happened?"

Aunt Gen nodded. "Oh yes. Ah, here's Silent with the tea tray. Did you see that I'd baked fresh biscuits? Good! Oh, and can you see if Raahi is here? I have good reason to be concerned about him."

Sie gave her aunt a look. "Concerned? Why?"

"After the close call with that snake, I went to visit an old friend today who used to be a professional seer. He's quite elderly, but he still sees a lot."

"And?" Sie prompted.

"He seems to think some dastardly plot is hatching. Hopefully it's nothing, but we ought to be careful."

"What, the CIA again?" Sie asked.

"Someone even more dangerous, if my friend is to be believed—but he wasn't sure who."

"That's not very helpful," Sie pointed out as she turned the key in the lock (there was again that sensation of flickering) and swung the door open.

Raahi wasn't there yet.

"Let's leave it open," Aunt Gen suggested. "It's a lovely afternoon. In both worlds," she added with a glance out the window, which showed a blue sky similar to the one visible through the side door. But the view out the window otherwise was not a close match, since there was a tall, modern building and a jet trail above it in the sky. Ali kept looking between the window and the open door.

"You seem amazed, Ali," Aunt Gen said. "Hasn't your Parallel Worlds class covered doorways yet? I should think it would be a basic concept. Something to teach in the very first lecture."

"Old Doors-and-Holes hasn't covered doors yet," Sie explained. "Or holes. Wardrobes, caves, magic ponds, but not your basic doorway—which is silly because that's how you usually enter another world. I mean, in the *real* world, right?"

"Quite so," Aunt Gen said. "Is your instructor Augie Dorsenhaal? He knows a lot about the ways between worlds. He was a Custodian until he took early retirement," she went on. "Didn't he mention that?"

The girls exchanged a surprised look.

"Well, you couldn't have a more qualified instructor," Aunt Gen said. "Now, would you please look for Raahi again?"

Sie nearly spilled her tea when she leaned out the door to look for him. "Wow!" she exclaimed. "I've never seen him run so fast! I hope he doesn't bump into—oh! He nearly smacked into that mailbox."

"He's probably being chased," Aunt Gen said, coming to her feet and hurrying over. Ali jumped up and joined them as Raahi ran up the block, his open blazer flapping and his schoolbag thumping awkwardly over his shoulder. "Get ready," Aunt Gen added. "You may have to weave a barrier spell to prevent our door from being breached by his pursuer."

Raahi bounced off a thickset man in a heavy overcoat, who turned to glare at him.

"He's almost here," Sie said. "But I can't see who's chasing him. They're probably concealed."

Aunt Gen nodded. "We'll need a concealment around our door, and I think a confusion behind Raahi would be helpful too."

SIX

The Race

"You do the confusion, Ali. I'll conceal the door," Sie said.

Raahi was nearing their gate. Aunt Gen pressed a hand on each of the girls' shoulders and said, "Now!"

Ali pointed at the street and shouted commands in a mixture of Greek and Latin while Sie raised her arms and muttered in ancient Avestan (obscure and difficult to work with but exceptionally strong).

"Raahi!" Aunt Gen called. "This way!" But her words were lost as chaos erupted out on the street. An elegant black motor car's engine exploded in a burst of oily smoke just behind Raahi. The driver, unable to see where he was going, swerved into a horse-drawn wagon carrying a load of lumber. The horse reared and the wagon tipped, dumping lumber on the sidewalk and street. An elegant carriage drawn by a well-groomed white horse was going the other way but as chaos broke out, the horse let out a terrified whinny and tried to turn around, blocking more cars and carriages and frightening pedestrians who dropped their packages and leapt over iron railings into the nearest gardens and yards.

Raahi spun around to survey the chaos behind him. He was breathing hard and sweat was running behind his thick glasses into his eyes, making it even harder to see than usual. However, what little he could see and everything he could hear—whinnies, shouts, bangs, thumps, and the crackle of a hot, oily fire—reassured him that his pursuer was going to have trouble getting through. He squinted toward the side door and raised a hand with two fingers in a V then sprinted away up Newbury Street.

There was an unfortunate moment in which Raahi seemed not to realize that a young couple was holding hands as he burst between them, but by the time they recovered enough for the man to shake his fist and curse at Raahi's retreating back, he was too far past them to care.

Something shifted hard. Aunt Gen's eyebrows rose. "Heavens! Is that yours, Sie?" she asked.

"It's the strongest concealment I know. There's no way anyone will see our side door now."

"Things are so hazy *I* can hardly see," Ali complained.

"I'll summon my field glasses," Gen said, putting a hand out. A second or two passed, and then a pair of old-fashioned brass binoculars appeared with a *pop.* "Here, Silent, see if you can find whoever was chasing him."

Sie focused the glasses and scanned the road. "There's a lot of smoke from that motor that blew up. What did you do, Ali?"

"I thought I was making fog," Ali said. "We read about it last year in our weavings class, remember?"

"Nobody's going to get past all *that*," Sie said, focusing on the toppled woodpile, the bucking horses, and the various disabled vehicles. "Wait, there's someone who wasn't there before," she added.

"A sorcerer?" Aunt Gen asked.

"A teenager."

"My friend the seer said something about a sorcerer," Aunt Gen said.

"This boy's out of breath like he's been running," Sie reported. "And, oh! He's jumped a railing and he's cutting through front gardens. Now he's running up Newbury again. Good thing Raahi's out of sight, but I'm still going to follow him." She handed the binoculars back to Aunt Gen.

"Who's the boy chasing Raahi?" Ali asked.

"Gray flannel pants and a blazer with a shield embroidered on the pocket. I can't see what it says, but it's red and orange, so he's probably from BAAM. Darn! Now he's disappeared again."

"Behind something?" Ali asked.

"His own concealment. He's good at them. I'm going after them now. Raahi needs help."

Aunt Gen held Silent back. "Not in the side door world," she said. "Come!" Swinging the door closed and signaling for Silent to lock it, she hurried to the front door and, pausing only to select a cane and a flowery hat, went down the steps onto busy, modern Newbury Street. "We should run," she said. "We have to get there in time to meet him."

"Where?" Ali asked rather breathlessly as they rushed up the block.

"Mr. Vose's gallery," Sie said. "That's what the V was for."

"I assume so," Aunt Gen agreed. "To avoid leading that boy to *our* door, he's aiming for the gallery's door. Smart. However, it would be best if he doesn't see the Vose door either. Now don't ask me anything more. I need my breath for running, dears."

Soon they were outside another old stone and brick house, this one with a set of wide steps leading up to a pair of blue-painted doors. A sign said: "Vose Gallery." They paused, scanning the street. The cheerful, crowded sidewalks held no hint of anything sinister. Modern traffic ground and honked its way up Newbury Street like normal.

"Hurry! We have to open the door for him," Sie said, and then she was racing up the steps to the gallery, Aunt Gen and Ali panting along after her.

Meanwhile, Raahi had bumped into a large woman carrying bulky shopping bags, stopped to offer a brief "Sorry!" then rushed onward, rubbing his elbow because one of the bags had held something bulky and hard. Like most people with limited vision, he didn't usually run on crowded sidewalks. When he finally reached Vose Gallery, he pushed through a small group of people in the front lobby and doubled over for a moment, panting.

"Are you lost?" a salesperson demanded. He was wearing a blue suit and a blue tie with large white polka dots. Even Raahi could see a pattern as bold as that one with ease. The man's voice hinted at a skeptical expression, no doubt a raised eyebrow or two, but since Raahi had just come in from the bright sunlight, he couldn't see the man's face; he could only guess at it.

"Uh, I'm here as an intern to a collector, but I'm late. He's upstairs," Raahi lied, then he hurried past the man and up the carpeted stairs to the second floor—where the side door he recalled from their previous adventure was located.

As he reached the landing and jogged down the hall toward the back room, he heard a commotion at the front door. "Wait just one minute, young man!" the salesman exclaimed. "We don't permit students to play tag in this establishment!"

Oh no! Raahi thought. *He's followed me in. I hope he didn't see me come upstairs!* And then he reached the door, except there wasn't a door there, just a blank wall with a small keyhole. The door would appear only if someone used a magical key in that hole, and Raahi did not have a key. He stood staring at the wall, wondering if Silent had understood his plan. If not, then the boy who was now arguing with the salesman would probably catch him.

That was the side-door-world version of the gallery. In the modern gallery, Silent, Ali, and Aunt Generous had just entered through the same blue doors. They found themselves alone in the carpeted front hall. There were people in various rooms, leaning forward to study the paintings. "Second floor," Sie said.

When they reached the room where the door was located, Aunt Gen stopped short and said, "Oh my!" She had not expected to stumble upon a large painting of herself, much younger, seated beside a tea tray, about to pour out a cup for a visitor.

"Hiding the door behind a painting of you," Sie explained, "is Mr. Vose's idea of humor, I imagine. Help me take it down, Ali."

"Would you like to purchase one of them?" someone asked. A young man with his hair slicked back, wearing a formal suit and brightly striped silk tie, had entered the room.

"We're just looking," Aunt Gen said. "And discussing the paintings amongst ourselves." When the salesman seemed not to get the hint, she added, "If we decide to make a purchase, you shall be the first to know. I presume we will be able to find you downstairs in the office?"

"Ah. Of course." He frowned. "I'll be waiting." He hurried off, leaving them alone in the room.

"Quickly," Aunt Gen said. "And by that I am *not* referring to my cousin Quick, although he was known in his day as something of a painter. He specialized in portraits of racehorses."

"Very funny," Sie said as they lifted the painting down.

"Well, he did. My, I'm heavy," Aunt Gen added as they carried the painting. "Lean me over here."

"I'm confused," Ali admitted.

"That's because you don't know about *this*." Sie pulled out her key and inserted it in a little brass keyhole that was set, oddly, in the bare wall where the painting had been hanging.

There was a shimmering and the floor vibrated beneath their feet. Where the wall had been bare, there was now a neatly framed doorway with a brass knob. Sie turned her key and reached for the knob. "Oh!" She stumbled back as someone on the other side threw open the door.

It was Raahi, his hair wild, beads of perspiration on his forehead and his glasses askew. "Hurry!" he cried as he swung the door closed. "Lock it!"

Sie turned her key in the lock again and the door disappeared.

"I—oh! Uh, hello there, sir." Raahi, having just stepped through, was facing away from the magical door and was the first to spot the salesman returning.

The man was followed closely by a middle-aged woman in an expensively simple blue dress. She cleared her throat and glared at them. "Why have you taken that painting down?" she demanded. "Only staff are allowed to touch paintings. If you wish to purchase one, we will wrap it for you. But *that* one is not for sale," she added. "Don't ask me why. I've grown quite tired of it, but the owners do not wish to part with it for some reason."

"I see your point," Aunt Gen said. "It's not as nice as I thought at first. We won't take it after all. Good day!" And then she swept past them, towing Sie, Ali, and Raahi in her wake.

"I don't know if he saw me come through the door," Raahi said, sounding breathless as they hurried out the front door. "He was in the gallery."

"He didn't get *through* the door," Sie said. "That's what matters most."

"But what if he saw it?" Raahi asked.

"Let's discuss this when we get home," Aunt Gen said. "Over a hot cup of tea. Silent, do you think you could do a remote ignition spell?"

"What, and light him on fire? Are you serious?" Sie looked shocked at the thought.

"Not the boy who chased Raahi, my dear. The teakettle. Our first pot is no doubt cold by now."

"Oh! Sure. Hold on." She let her eyelids flutter closed as she visualized the kitchen stove and the big old kettle, dents and all. There was a *whoosh* as the gas burner beneath the kettle lit. She opened her eyes. "It's going now," she reported.

"Very good. Here!" Aunt Gen raised an arm and waved a fluttering white handkerchief, and suddenly there was a shiny black Model T pulling up to the curb, its long rear addition offering varnished oak benches with green velvet cushions.

"Miss Lee," the driver said, tipping his cap. "Good to see you again. Home?"

"Thank you, yes. Come along, young people. Hop in. We don't want the tea water to boil away."

SEVEN

The Hunt Club

They were seated in comfortable chairs around a tea tray in Aunt Gen's parlor. Raahi was telling his story. "When school ended today, that jerk who chased me came up to me with three others and, well, they pushed me against a wall." Here Raahi paused to feel his stomach. "Two of them held my arms, and the other two punched me."

"Raahi! Are you hurt?" Sie leaned forward.

"I whispered a ward in time to protect myself from the worst of the attack," Raahi said. "Good thing I'd read about blocking wards over the summer."

"I thought you said you couldn't do magic," Sie said.

"I'm terrible in class, but the things I study on my own go better."

"I wonder if someone is putting an interference on you when you're in class," Aunt Gen said. "We'll have to look into that."

"Why would they do that?" Raahi asked.

"They might not want you to succeed as a student," Aunt Gen said.

"I've only been there two days! How could I have made so many enemies?"

"That's a very good question," Sie said. "Did they say anything that might explain what they're up to?"

"The one who chased me, Rudy, got right up in my face and hissed, 'Tell us how you do it or we'll turn you into dog meat.' By 'do it,' I believe he meant how I cross between neighboring worlds. I didn't want to be interrogated further, so I muddled them with a confusion influence. Unfortunately, Rudy shook off the influence and pursued me."

"A confusion influence?" Sie asked. "Did you read about that over the summer too?"

"In the books you lent me."

"How do you think they figured out that you're from another world?" Sie continued.

Raahi shrugged.

"Did you talk about side doors?" Ali asked.

"Definitely not!" Raahi exclaimed.

"I'm sure you were appropriately discrete," Aunt Gen said. "And by that, I'm not referring to my Great Uncle Appropriate." Sie rolled her eyes. "However, *something* tipped them off."

"Well . . ." Raahi frowned. "Yesterday morning I put on a sweater. When I got to school I hung it up in my locker, but it was gone at the end of the day. I found it this morning in the lost and found. This is it. I'm wearing it now."

"Where is it from?" Aunt Gen asked.

"Macy's. It's navy blue like the school dress code says."

"Oh dear," Aunt Gen said.

"What?" Raahi looked worried.

"It's probably got a label," Sie said.

"And it might have modern synthetics in it," Aunt Gen added.

"The tiny little label on the inside of the neck?" Raahi asked, sounding surprised. "Those have such small writing they aren't even legible. Well, to me, anyway," he added.

Sie got up and tugged at the neck of his sweater to reveal the label. "Made in Bangladesh," she read. "Of seventy percent wool and thirty percent Lycra. That's a modern fiber, isn't it?"

"Yes," Aunt Gen said.

"I didn't think," Raahi said. "And, sorry, but I believe Bangladesh was established in 1971 when the independence fighters defeated the British. The name isn't used in the side door world."

"Bangla-what?" Ali asked then flushed. She was still feeling shy around Raahi, and to make it worse, she couldn't stop herself from glancing at him.

"I'll take the label out. Can I borrow some scissors?" Raahi asked.

"You should wear clothes from the side door world," Sie said. "That's what we do. Auntie, we'll have to take him shopping. Saturday?"

"No, he will skip morning classes tomorrow and shop with me, then I'll drop him at school. I need to have a word with the headmaster anyway. Things are getting serious at BAAM."

"Can *we* help with the shopping?" Ali asked. "It would give us an excuse to skip Doors-and-Holes's lecture."

"I'm sorry," Raahi said. "I didn't realize."

"Normally no one would notice," Aunt Gen said, "which means someone is looking especially hard for reveals. An odd thing to do, unless . . ."

"Unless what?" Sie asked. "Do you know who it is?"

"I hope not. Perhaps it's more innocent than the last time something like this happened."

"You're being cryptic," Sie complained.

"Who else was punching you?" Ali interjected. "I know a lot of your classmates, but I *hope* they wouldn't act like *that*."

"I don't know the rest of their names, but they're in some club," Raahi said.

Aunt Gen leaned forward. "And what is the name of this club?"

"The Hunt Club. I heard them say that," Raahi said, "but I don't know what they hunt."

"I do." Aunt Gen frowned. "They were a secret club that was stamped out decades ago after causing a *lot* of trouble."

"What sort of trouble?" Sie asked.

"They snuck into parallel worlds and stole objects of power," Aunt Gen said.

"To become more powerful themselves?" Raahi guessed.

"Precisely. Otherworld forms of magic are so much harder to block," Aunt Gen explained. "No one knows the counters."

"But why," Ali asked, "would students need to be that powerful?"

"Most students just want to prepare for their careers," Aunt Gen said. "However, there are occasionally a twisted few whose plan is to take over the world after they graduate."

"Are you joking, Miss Lee?" Ali asked.

"No. I still recall the Hunt Club's motto: *Ad capere mundum.*"

"To conquer the world," Sie translated.

"So, not just schoolyard bullies?" Raahi asked.

"Not your garden variety, no," Aunt Gen said. "Power-hungry maniacs and their impressionable followers, I'd guess. If their secret club has been revived, I'd be *very* careful."

Raahi frowned but did not say anything more. He thought it would be rude to point out that it was Aunt Gen who had arranged for him to go to BAAM in the first place—and now, after only two days, she was telling him how incredibly dangerous it was.

"How were they stopped the first time?" Sie asked.

"We tracked them to Egypt," Aunt Gen said, "and interrupted them before they could complete their delivery of otherworld weapons. Are you done, my dears? I think it's time for Ali and Raahi to be heading home."

"Is it safe for Ali to walk around the city right now?" Sie asked. "Seeing as the Hunt Club is based in her world?"

"Perhaps not. Let's hail a station hack for her. It really *is* the most accommodating mode of travel."

"How come whenever you call a taxi, the same one shows up?" Sie asked. "And with the same man at the wheel?"

"Another good question," Aunt Gen said. "Don't forget your book bag, Ali. I doubt Silent wants to do your homework."

"Or mine," Raahi said. "For all I know, it's about to be turned into tarantulas or something."

"I think," Aunt Gen said, "that whatever they tried to turn your homework into is going to crawl out of *their* book bags, and it will serve them right." She smiled.

But Raahi, Ali, and Sie exchanged a worried look. It occurred to them that the bullies at BAAM might blame Raahi for anything Aunt Gen's stone did to them.

EIGHT

Secrets

Silent opened the side door and led the way down the steps and through the garden. *No snakes,* she thought. *At least that's an improvement.*

Aunt Gen had barely raised her hand when the old-fashioned taxi *putt-putted* up to the curb and the same elderly driver touched his hat and said, "Good afternoon, Miss Lee. Where to this time?"

Ali climbed in as Aunt Gen exchanged a few whispered words with the driver. Sie overheard "keep her safe" and "they're back again," so she could guess what they were talking about. After the Model T motor sputtered into action and the taxi disappeared down Newbury Street, Sie, Raahi, and Aunt Gen turned to go back in the side gate. But Aunt Gen paused for a moment, looking at the front of the house. "Sometimes I miss those days," she said, sounding wistful.

"Which days, ma'am?" Raahi asked.

"When I was a, ah, professional weaver." She gestured toward the front porch. Beside the door, where there was nothing but a doorbell in the modern world, there was now a smooth brass plate with her name and profession on it: Generous Lee, W.O.R.L.D., Beneficial Weavings, *by appointment only.*

"We never go in the front door when we're in the side world," Silent explained to Raahi. "Aunt Gen's too young and way too busy." She glanced at her aunt. "And not always as friendly as she is now. Retirement suits you, Auntie," she quipped.

"I suppose it does. Let's step into the side garden," Aunt Gen added. "A client approaches."

"A client?" Raahi adjusted his glasses and stared as an impressive light blue carriage pulled up in front of the house, drawn by two magnificent horses. The coachman set the butt of his long whip into a holder, looped his reins around it, lowered a set of steps, and opened the carriage door.

A plump, tearful woman burst out of the carriage, clutching layers of ruffled mauve skirts in one hand and using her other hand to dab her cheek with a lacy bit of silk. She was wearing lace-up leather boots with such high heels that she nearly fell as she stepped onto the curb (the coachman offered a steadying arm). Then she tucked her handkerchief away in the fluffy lace of one sleeve, squared her shoulders, and set off up the front walk.

"It's Mrs. Cabot-Wallingford-Lodge. Worried about her daughters, I believe. They're going on a trip by steamship with stops in all the fashionable places. I made them safe-travel amulets. There were so many frivolous clients to deal with back then! It's nice to be retired."

"I thought you said you missed those days," Sie said.

"Ah." Aunt Gen paused. "Well, actually, not so much the days spent pretending to have a respectable career selling minor charms and weavings."

"Then, if you don't mind my asking, Ms. Lee," Raahi said, "what is it that you *do* miss?"

"I was, shall we say, a roving problem solver," Aunt Gen said.

"Who did you work for?" Raahi asked.

"Good luck getting any details out of her," Sie commented.

"It's still classified," Aunt Gen said. "Now, shall we go back in and send Raahi out the front door? His mother will worry if he's late for dinner."

"Can I just ask," Raahi continued, "what those letters after your name mean?"

"Oh, just a degree." Aunt Gen waved an airy hand in the general direction of the brass plate. "An old, musty college degree. Probably not even recognized anymore. I don't think they give them out very often these days."

"Didn't you study in England?" Sie asked. "At Oxford?"

"Yes, but Oxford's not the same as in the modern world," Aunt Gen said. "I lived in the side door world until I retired. In those days, we 'betweeners' were encouraged to choose one world and stay in it. Not very open minded back then. Or now, actually, but it's not such an issue because there are so few betweeners these days. You are *quite* special, my dears. Most people can't go between worlds regularly without side effects. It's very hard on them."

Raahi raised an eyebrow, but Silent whispered, "Don't worry. You'll be fine."

They entered through the side door and Sie turned to lock it as Aunt Gen took a sip from her neglected teacup. "Cold," she reported. "Shall we work on dinner? I picked up some iced mackerel right from the docks, and my greengrocer had fresh bunches of young salsify roots and shoots. We'll sauté the greens in butter and fry some cakes from the shredded tubers. Would you like to stay for dinner, Raahi? We could send a message to your mother."

"She'll be cooking for me," he said, "but I'd like to try your cooking sometime. It sounds like it's straight from the previous century."

Aunt Gen smiled. "Well," she said as Raahi slung his bag over his shoulder, "I hear your mother is quite the cook. Now, *do* keep an eye out on the walk home, although I doubt they've found a way into your world since they seem to be searching for doors. Still, one can't be too cautious."

"I'll walk him home," Sie said. "You don't really need help with dinner. You just like to pretend you do, so you can teach me old-fashioned cooking."

"How perceptive of you." Aunt Gen smiled. "Go ahead but come straight back. It'll be dark soon."

Sie headed toward the front door with Raahi. "Oh, and when I get back, I want to discuss my parentage," she added. "I still don't know a few of the more minor details. Like who my mother and father were."

Sie waited at the door for a reply, but Aunt Gen had already gone back into the kitchen. Rolling her eyes, she joined Raahi on the front porch and latched the door behind them.

"Is that true?" Raahi asked.

"That she won't tell me who my parents are? Yes. And another thing." Sie frowned.

"What?" Raahi asked.

"You know how I carry the Lee family key?" She patted her sweater where the key hung discretely out of sight under her blouse. "The thing is, Auntie seems to be able to go to the side door world without it."

"How?" Raahi looked puzzled. "I thought there were only a few doors in the entire city."

"You don't go to the docks and buy mackerel off a boat in *modern* Boston, and if you asked for salsify greens at the grocery store, they'd think you're nuts. But when I'm around, she acts like we can't go anywhere without my key."

"I think," Raahi said thoughtfully, "that if you spend your entire career doing things in secret, it must be hard to break the habit."

Sie frowned. "I couldn't trust my so-called mother because she was a spy, but at least I grew up trusting my aunt. I hope being a magical spy doesn't mean *she's* untrustworthy too."

"*Confide tibi*," Raahi said. It was a Latin saying that meant "Trust yourself."

NINE

Attacked

As they wove through the crowd of well-dressed shoppers, spa-goers, and restaurant diners along modern Newbury Street, Raahi said, "Do you know what your aunt's degree is? We only saw the letters."

Sie paused to let a woman with a large shopping bag go by. "It's from the Linacre Institute of Sorcery at Oxford. Her diploma's hanging in her study. The letters stand for 'World Order of the Royal Linacre Degree of Sorcery.'"

"If that's her actual degree," Raahi said, "then why did she leave the 'S' for sorcery off her plaque? It said W.O.R.L.D., but it should be W.O.R.L.D.S."

"I never thought of that," Sie said. "A mistake?" But knowing her aunt, she did not think so.

"Maybe it's a special college for people who can go between worlds, but they don't want anyone to know," Raahi said. "That would be my guess. 'Betweeners.' And there's something else odd about her degree too."

"Has anyone ever told you it's possible to be *too* smart?" Sie asked.

"You," Raahi said. "But think about it. Why is it 'World Order' instead of just 'Order'?"

"Because students come from all over the world?" Sie guessed.

"I don't think so. The use of 'world' is unnecessarily repeated."

"No, it's not," Sie said firmly.

"It's nested inside the W.O.R.L.D. acronym. Like, uh, matryoshka dolls. Actually, more like the Dutch artist Maurits Cornelis Escher's 'strange loop' drawings," Raahi continued, "where you go endlessly around a staircase, or where one hand comes out of the page to draw another that's coming out of the page to draw the first hand, which of course seems impossible. They call them *strange* loops because they violate the hierarchy of a nested system, suggesting another rule at work, perhaps magic."

"Raahi!"

"My point is—"

"Endless, as usual," Sie teased. "You're like a dragon chasing its own tail. But I get the gist if it. Multiple worlds. So what? Turn at this corner."

"It's another clue that they might specialize in interworld magic."

"You could've just said that. It's probably where Custodians were trained," Sie said.

Raahi stopped in the middle of the sidewalk. "Yes, but something's making the hair on the back of my neck stand up," he said, frowning.

"*That's* a nice visual. I'm not sure I wanted to know that."

"It's an expression. Don't you feel it?"

"You're right," Sie said, frowning. "Let's get under this roof." They were at the corner of Essex and Boylston, where a hotel entry offered convenient shelter. Raahi allowed Sie to draw him beneath its protection. People were coming and going and a man in uniform was stacking luggage on a cart.

"I've never been inside the Lenox Hotel," Raahi said.

"Me neither," Silent said, "but it's the nearest shelter and—*hey!*" she exclaimed as lightning sizzled into a fire hydrant a short distance from them, followed by a stunningly loud clap of thunder. The hydrant started to spray water. "Quick!" Sie cried, hurrying them through the glass doors.

And that is how they found themselves sheltering in the lobby of the Lenox Hotel as dusk came on and the red lights and loud siren of a fire truck approached.

"More mayhem," Raahi commented, "and Ali isn't even here. By the way, do you think she likes m—"

"Someone's weaving weather-workings," Sie interrupted, frowning. "I felt a pulse of magic just before that lightning struck."

"Was it aimed at *us?*" Raahi asked, alarmed.

"Well . . . I've almost been hit by falling branches and a large statue," Sie pointed out. "Auntie was nearly bitten by a viper, and you were beaten up and chased. Now *this.*"

"Oh dear. Do you think someone's trying to get your key again?"

Sie shrugged. "Someone's after us for *some* reason," she said. "As if starting ninth grade isn't enough to deal with."

They were standing in the middle of an ornate lobby with square white columns rising up to elaborately decorated ceiling panels. The walls were covered in wallpaper of a deep red and gold pattern. A pleasingly bright fire flickered from a large fireplace on one wall.

"We don't exactly blend in," Raahi pointed out, "but at least we're in our school clothes. It's no place for T-shirts."

"I don't own any T-shirts," Sie said. "They're a modern world thing. That's strange!" she added, turning to stare.

"What?" Raahi asked.

"One of my teachers just came out that door on the other side of the lobby where it says 'City Bar.'"

An older man in a tan overcoat, his hair a halo of white, was coming toward them. He moved quickly, which was surprising because in class he barely moved at all. He was Sie's Parallel Worlds instructor, Master Dorsenhaal.

"Are you Gen's daughter?" he demanded, looking at her over his glasses.

"Niece. She's my great aunt. Don't you recognize me from class?"

"Ah, sorry, my mistake. And this is the boy the Custodian told me about, I presume. Come!" He turned and hurried across the lobby.

"Boy?" Raahi repeated, offended.

"What are you doing here?" Sie demanded, hurrying to catch up with Master Dorsenhaal. "This isn't even the same *world* as GALA."

"No time to explain. Please hurry!" He gestured for them to follow him.

They had reached the elevators. One was open, and Master Dorsenhaal stepped into it. Raahi, who had just caught up with them, exchanged a puzzled look with Sie.

"I think it's all right," she said as she stepped into the elevator, tugging Raahi after her.

As her instructor pushed the button, Sie said, "My name is Silent. Don't you recognize me from class, sir? You took attendance just this morning."

"The whole name or just some of the letters?"

"Huh?"

"Are silent. Wait, your actual *name* is Silent?"

"I sat in the back row today."

"You assume I know you from class, but the truth is that I haven't taught for a very long time. Dreadfully dull."

"If you aren't her teacher, then who *are* you?" Raahi demanded.

Sie frowned and blocked the door from closing. "A double?"

"Worried about illusions?" Master Dorsenhaal asked. "Very sensible, but this is not the time." He tugged Sie toward him. She lost her grip on the door and it dinged closed.

"Hey!" Raahi exclaimed.

Sie didn't say anything, but as the elevator began to ascend, she traced something with a fingertip in the air.

"*Uh!*" The man seemed startled. He shook his head, took off his glasses, rubbed his eyes, and put his glasses back on. "I've been struck by a powerful working, haven't I?"

"What did you use on him?" Raahi asked.

"A compulsion to truth," the man said before Sie could answer. "*Veritatem semper et tantum*, I believe. A difficult working and *far* above student level. Impressive."

"Who are you?" Sie demanded.

"I *am* Master Dorsenhaal," he said. "Your compulsion forces me to be honest. Now, if you would please remove it? It's rather itchy, I'm afraid."

Sie glanced at Raahi then waved her hand.

"I don't blame you for wanting to be sure," Master Dorsenhaal added, smiling for the first time.

"Then who's giving those boring lectures?" Sie demanded. "Do you have a twin?"

"Hah! In a way I do. A deeply woven illusion that discharges my duties so I don't have to, but please don't spread that around school! Here we are, top floor," he said as the button marked "11" lit up and the elevator bell rang.

And then he was hurrying into the hall (also ornately decorated and trimmed) and down to a corner room, where he extracted a key—it was hanging on a string, just like Silent's—and turned it in the lock.

Raahi said, "This hotel seems so old fashioned."

"It's one of those buildings," Sie said, "that date back to the same era as the side door world. Which means there may be a side door here," she added, thinking of the key Master Dorsenhaal had used. She'd noticed that all the other doors on the hall had modern card-readers instead of traditional locks.

Master Dorsenhaal was holding the door for them. Moving cautiously and looking all around, they entered. There was a faint tingling as they went in, suggestive of magic at work.

"Make yourselves comfortable," Master Dorsenhaal said. "It's a rather spacious suite. Oh, and Silent? I'm on the same telephone exchange as Generous. You may call her. And I *think* the modern phone on the desk will reach your mother, young man," he added as Raahi entered. "If you know how to work it. I don't."

Indeed there were two phones. The one on the wall was large, black, and very old fashioned. A more modern one sat on a desk in the main room.

They paused, staring around them. The room was comfortably furnished with old-fashioned leather chairs and couches, and there were tall windows overlooking the Boston cityscape. Oddly, although the Prudential Center and other modern buildings should have been visible, the view out the widows was of the side door world. The Lenox seemed to be the tallest building.

"I prefer this landscape," Master Dorsenhaal said as he opened a large closet to hang up his overcoat. Sie was surprised to see that there were numerous overcoats already on hangers. She wondered if he lived in the hotel full time. "But if you wish to see contemporary Boston, just close the blinds, then reopen them. The view toggles back and forth."

"Does the building itself toggle back and forth?" Sie asked.

"Just this suite. Now, why don't you two warm yourselves and get rid of that dampness? There's a fire in the hearth." And indeed there was a crackling wood fire in an old-fashioned fireplace, which seemed very out of place in modern Boston.

"I'll call Auntie, if you don't mind," Sie said.

"Be my guest."

Sie put the receiver to her mouth. "Hello? Operator? Can you connect me with Generous Lee on Newbury?"

"Of course, dear. I'll ring her now. Hold on a sec."

After a short wait, Aunt Gen's voice came on the line. "Hello?"

"It's me, Auntie. We're at the Lenox Hotel. We bumped into Master Doors-and, I mean, Dorsenhaal, and he brought us up to his room. Do you think it's safe?" As she said this, she cupped her hand over the mouthpiece and lowered her voice.

"He's as safe as they get. I suppose you've discovered his secret, then?"

"That he uses an illusion to read his notes?"

"Hah! Well, you mustn't gossip, not even to Ali. Now, what's happened?"

"Someone used storm magic and tried to electrocute us."

"Lightning? That's *strictly* forbidden. I used to draw the magic out of sorcerers for less. Are you all right?"

"We're fine. We took shelter here."

"Hmm. Well, you're safe enough with Dorsenhaal, I think. I'll send the hack to pick you up. I . . . oh, dear! Someone's at the door."

"What do you mean?"

"The *side* door, Silent. They're knocking on it. I don't think that's ever happened before."

"Someone with a lot of power then," Sie said. "My concealment's still there. Don't open it!"

"I won't, but . . . goodness! That was a big lightning strike. And now they're pounding on the front door. Perhaps you had better stay with Master—" *CRACK! Szzzzzz.* The line went dead.

"Raahi!" Sie cried. "Something's happening at Aunt Gen's!"

"I've got to go, Maa," Raahi hurried to say into the modern telephone. "I'll be home eventually, I promise." He hung up. "What's happened?"

"Something bad," Sie said. "I have to go home right now."

"Young woman, you shall do no such thing." Master Dorsenhaal emerged from a back room with a small suitcase in hand. "I've just been packing. Too bad you didn't have time to gather a few things."

"Packing?" She stared at him. "Why?"

"Because Boston is no longer safe." He glanced at an old-fashioned pocket watch before slipping it back into his vest pocket. "People are chasing you around modern Boston at the same time someone is pounding on your aunt's side door and trying to shoot you with lightning. We can deduce that there is a plot of rather large dimensions. And I *don't* like the look of the weather," he added, glancing out the window, where lightning flashed wildly across the cityscape.

"Where do you propose we go?" Raahi asked.

"For starters, the closet. If you'll poke around in the back of it, I'm almost certain you'll find overcoats that fit you. You're going to need them." He opened the closet door and gestured for them to step in.

They exchanged surprised glances, but rain had begun to spatter the windowpanes. Raahi said, "Why not?" and pushed some too-large overcoats aside. There was another row. He pressed in, reaching for one, but it also seemed too large. "Here, help me, Sie. There's not enough light."

Sie pushed in after him. It was surprisingly deep for a coat closet, but Master Dorsenhaal was right; there were more rows of coats. She tugged one off its hanger for herself and a slightly bigger one for Raahi.

"Hey, watch out!" she exclaimed. Master Dorsenhaal had come in, pulling the door closed behind him, and his suitcase was bumping her back.

"It's just a few more steps," he said, his voice sounding at once close to her ear and oddly muffled by coats. "Young man, do you feel another door?"

"I'm Raahi, and I don't appreciate being closed into . . . oh! Yes, in fact there *is* a door. How Lewisian. Shall I open it?"

"At once. I hear someone knocking on the outer door to my suite."

"This is your escape route?" Sie asked as hinges creaked and a slice of light opened to a full rectangle up ahead. "Where does it go?"

"It's someone's apartment, I think," Raahi said from up ahead.

"What about Aunt Gen?" Sie demanded, pausing in the midst of the overcoats.

Master Dorsenhaal nudged her toward the new door. "Not now," he said. "We can't help her if we get caught or killed ourselves."

"Someone's breaking into her house!" Sie turned and pushed back to the first door again.

However, as she was reaching for the knob, a tremendous clap of thunder shook the floor and made the coats flap on their hangers as the door lit up with a brilliant sizzle.

She did not know what happened after that.

TEN

Toads

Silent sat up, blinking. She was on an unfamiliar floor in front of a coat closet. Raahi was leaning over her, looking very worried. "Are you all right?" he asked.

"What happened?" She tried to get up but was too dizzy. She spoke a revival chant and tried again. Although still unsteady, she was able to stand.

"They blew the door in on you," Raahi explained. "Your professor warded us while I pulled you through."

Sie hurried over to the closet door. It was locked. She spoke an opening. Nothing happened. She tried a more powerful working, but still nothing. She frowned. "Master Dorsenhaal?" she called.

"He went upstairs with his suitcase," Raahi said. "I think he's unpacking."

"What about Aunt Gen?"

Raahi frowned.

She tried the door again, this time using an even stronger chant. Still nothing. As she was stepping back and raising her arms to summon a wind and smash it, Raahi cleared his throat.

"What?"

"I don't think it's going to open," Raahi said. "I believe it's full of stone all the way through. To keep them out, he said."

"A concretion? Darn! That would've destroyed the portal. Where are we?"

"I'm not sure," Raahi said.

"We better still be in Boston," Sie said.

She looked around. They were in an entry hall leading into an old-fashioned sitting room, complete with gaslights on the walls instead of electric. Beyond the sitting room and through a pair of glass doors, they could see a small kitchen with a black iron stove and a marble-topped worktable. In the other direction, another set of multipaned doors opened onto what looked like a cozy library. Through yet a third set of doors, stairs curved up out of sight.

"Do hang up your overcoats, but not in the closet, sorry. Try the coatrack over there." Master Dorsenhaal had just emerged from the staircase. "I expect I have some fizzy drinks in the icebox, although the ice will have melted because I haven't been here for a while. And there ought to be an assortment of biscuits in the larder. Help yourselves." And then he turned and disappeared up the stairs again.

"Why's he talking like that?" Sie asked, staring after him.

"My mother calls cookies biscuits and sodas fizzies," Raahi said. "She moved from London when I was a baby." He polished his glasses and peered out the nearest window.

"Did we leave Boston?" Sie asked, frowning.

"Early morning light, heavy clouds and rain, funny words. Sorry, Sie, but I think we're in England. And the gaslights and icebox suggest we're back in side door time."

"England? Darn! But that explains the daylight," Sie said. "It was evening a minute ago."

"I assume we're in a different time zone."

"Very different," Master Dorsenhaal said, reemerging from the staircase. "It's early morning here. Hope you weren't tired," he added. "We bypassed sleep."

"What about Aunt Gen?" Sie demanded.

"That's what you were saying just before you were knocked out," Master Dorsenhaal replied. "Do you have to be so persistent? It's bad for your health."

"I'm worried about her. I need to go back." She was standing with her hands on her hips. "Now."

Master Dorsenhaal nodded. "I understand your concern," he said, "but the best I can do is to take you to my college. We have doors there. Will that do?"

"How far is it?" Sie demanded.

"Walking distance. Won't you sit down and have some refreshment first?"

"No. Where exactly are we?" Sie insisted.

"Saint Cross Road, Oxford, just across from Linacre College. Welcome to England. I keep a flat here."

"Is this *my* side door world?" Sie asked.

"Yes. However, to get back to Boston the way normal people do would involve a trip by train to Liverpool and then a steamship to Boston."

"We need to go there today," Sie said. "Preferably right now."

"Of course," Master Dorsenhaal said.

Raahi had gone into the kitchen. "Something to drink?" he called.

"No," Sie said as she put on her overcoat again.

"I'll take a fizzy. Whatever you can find," Master Dorsenhaal said. "And then we'll go."

"How's this, Master D?" Raahi asked, bringing him a cola in a glass.

Master Dorsenhaal smiled. "I suppose, Raahi, that if I actually showed up to teach, I might earn a more affectionate nickname than Old Doors-and-Holes. And Dorsenhaal *is* a mouthful, isn't it?"

"You don't mind 'Master D,' then?" Raahi asked. "It kind of slipped out. I wasn't really thinking."

"It will do, thanks, and so will the drink, although not normally recommended for breakfast."

"Why are you delaying?" Sie was standing by the front door.

"Too early," Master D said. "Linacre College doesn't open its gate for another twenty minutes. Not the modern college—it wasn't established until the 1970s—but the side door version. It goes way back, some say before Oxford University itself."

"Do you think she's all right?" Sie asked.

"She knows what to do in an emergency," Master D said, "but just in case, I sent a message to the Boston Custodian." He took another sip of his soda. "And I promise I'll get you home soon."

"As soon as possible, please. By the way, how did you happen to be at the Lenox?" Sie examined him thoughtfully.

Master Dorsenhaal shrugged. "I was, shall we say, on duty."

"On duty?" Sie repeated, eyebrows raised.

He leaned forward and lowered his voice. "I'm retired from active duty but I'm still on call. That chase up Newbury Street caught the local Custodian's eye. I was following you on his behalf."

"No, you weren't," Raahi said. "You were already at the hotel, weren't you?"

"We saw you at the bar," Sie added.

"I was following you in an anticipatory fashion," he said. "Best to keep a step ahead."

"Wait, you *knew* we'd go into the hotel?" Sie stared at him. "How?"

"Oh, well, you see . . ." He pulled out his pocket watch and flipped open the silver lid.

They leaned over to stare at the face. As well as the normal minute and hour hands, several other hands spun around smaller dials. One of them was marked with levels of magical activity from low to very high, another had threat levels ("Duck," "Prepare to duck," "Coming your way," and "Maybe tomorrow" were some of the words Sie could read), and a third was marked "Proximity Alignment: Here and Now, Incoming, There and Then."

"It's an anticipatory clock. It helps me know when and where important things will take place," Master D explained.

"Like attacks?" Raahi asked.

"Quite so."

"Then where were you when that bolt of lightning almost got us?" Sie asked.

"I thought the threat would be more minor, since I assumed the trouble was caused by students. *That* attack was the work of a highly trained sorcerer. No student could bring lightning down with such speed and precision."

"Actually, I know one student who—" Raahi began.

He was recalling how Sie had done something quite similar on their last adventure, but Sie gripped his arm and said, "Let's not go into that. So, you went to the bar and waited?"

Master D nodded. "But when I heard the sirens, I came to see what had happened."

"That still doesn't explain the coincidence of our being driven right into the lobby of the same hotel where you keep a room," Raahi pointed out.

"No, it doesn't." Master D glanced at the watch again then slipped it away. "Sometimes this watch is not so much anticipating the future as influencing it."

"Influencing?" Sie repeated. "Did it *make* someone attack us?" she asked, her eyes narrowing.

"The watch's peculiar magic is to bring such events to me as well as me to them. If I hadn't used the watch to track you, your magical hit man might have made his move somewhere else along your route. Once I opened the watch, then the possibilities began to be pulled together until you, your attacker, and I became proximate. That's how it works. A sort of gathering of possibilities. We TOADs were, all of us, trained to use these."

"The illusionary you likes to lecture too," Sie said. "But back to the main question. Why were you following us and who exactly *are* you?"

"A toad?" Raahi asked.

"Yes. That's what they do here at Linacre College. Train us."

"I'm still vague on what small, brown amphibians have to do with our current predicament," Raahi said.

"It stands for one of the more exciting and dangerous professions in all of the worlds: *Tandem Openings Abuse Deterrence*. Tandem is an old-fashioned word for parallel worlds. Openings are ways between worlds. I'm a Custodian. Didn't you know?"

"Cus-TOAD-ian! Hah, that's clever," Raahi said. "So Custodian is just a nickname and the real term is, uh, tandem et cetera?"

"Yes. We're an independent interworld agency dedicated to *securitas mundi*, the security of the worlds."

"You don't work for the government?" Raahi asked.

Master D shook his head. "Sometimes we must work against governments, in fact."

"I think he's wondering who employs you," Sie said. "Which is a very good question, seeing as it will determine whether we trust you or not." She eyed him pointedly.

"We are affiliated with the college and funded by it. The college was established to protect world boundaries."

"So you're telling us that Custodians are vigilantes?" Raahi asked. "Meting out justice as they see fit?"

Master Dorsenhaal's eyebrow arched expressively. Then he began to laugh. "Magical vigilantes, my my!" He chuckled. "Hah! But I hope we are a bit more disciplined and cautious than some posse from your Wild West movies." He turned to Sie. "Has anyone told him that it's possible to be *too* clever?"

"Perhaps."

"I see." He smiled.

"Uh, can I try my aunt on your phone?" Sie asked. She'd noticed another old-fashioned wall phone tucked into a corner of the kitchen.

"Alas, they have yet to install a trunk line beneath the Atlantic. You could write."

"Darn!" Sie frowned. "All right, I guess we believe you about being a frog or whatever," she went on. "But why leave my aunt in danger?"

"The Custodian from the Boston Public Library was hurrying to her even as I was whisking you out of harm's way. We divided and, well, escaped, I trust." He flashed her a reassuring smile. "And perhaps you know something of your aunt's training. She's quite capable."

"She was on a CRACK team, yes. But that was a long time ago," Sie said with a frown.

"Can you check with the Custodian?" Raahi asked. "Just to be sure?"

"It's PP right now. That stands for 'Paranoia Protocol.' We won't be communicating for fear of being overheard."

"Because you don't know the extent of the enemy's capabilities?" Raahi asked.

"Precisely. They seem to be strangely well informed. Inside help, I'd guess."

"PP? Why does everybody use these stupid acronyms," Sie grumbled.

"All right, I think we can go," Master D said. "It's almost seven." And with that, he swung the front door open and they stepped out into the Oxford weather.

ELEVEN

Eternal Breakfast

Saint Cross Road was empty except for a horse pulling a milk cart over the wet cobblestones. Dodging puddles as they crossed, they aimed for an iron gate beneath an arch.

As they neared, a weathered-looking man in brown country tweeds swung the gate open then picked up a bamboo fishing rod and a wicker basket with a leather strap, which he slung over his shoulder. "Chub'll be nibblin' when this precipitation abates," he said with a wide smile that revealed several missing front teeth. And then he disappeared down a path to their right.

"Groundskeeper," Master D explained. "Been here since I was a student. Opens the gate every morning and locks it every evening. Never ill, never takes a day off, never goes on vacation."

"And never misses a chance to fish?" Raahi added.

Master D smiled. "I suppose not. He seems to treat the college more like a club than a job. But you have to admire his enthusiasm, and he's a regular wizard with that fishing pole. He'll bring a bucket of fish to the kitchen and they'll serve fillets for lunch."

"Is there a pond on campus?" Sie asked as they headed up a brick walk toward a tall brick building.

"River. The Cherwell runs behind the college on the far side of a wooded park."

"Hard to believe this is a college," Sie said as they walked toward what looked more like a very large brick house. "And it sure is quiet," she added.

"When I was young, it was a bustling place with dozens of students. Now the program is halfway shut down, but there's still a core group of masters here. It's hard to find students because betweeners are growing ever more rare. In my day, you'd see students all over the grounds, practicing their workings and weavings."

"You have to be a betweener to be a Custodian?" Raahi asked. "I guess that makes sense," he added, answering his own question. "Is this the main entrance?"

Master D was just reaching for the door knocker when a sizzling sound made them look up. The clouds above them flashed with electricity.

"Hurry!" Raahi cried as a dart of lightning struck the brick path a few yards from them, scattering red-brown chips that stung their legs.

Master D banged the knocker loudly.

There was no answer, but the cloud began to buzz with energy again.

"Excuse me," Sie said, elbowing Master D aside and muttering as she cupped her hands over the doorknob. The door creaked open, revealing a dark and dusty wood-paneled entry hall. They hurried in and slammed the door behind them as another clap of thunder rent the air and heavier rain began to pelt down, streaking the triangular windowpanes on either side of the door.

"Like I was saying, you never know when you'll need an overcoat," Master D commented as he took his off and hung it on one of the hooks in a row beside the door.

"And you never know when the weather might try to *kill* you," Raahi complained.

"Is it always this deserted?" Sie asked. The hall was empty and quiet.

"Maybe they're at breakfast," Master D suggested, but he frowned and bit his lip as they kicked up dust along the empty hall.

After leading them down several corridors, he stopped in front of a wide door. It was slightly ajar.

He put a finger to his lips and peeked through the crack.

His eyebrows shot up and he took a startled step back. "Oh dear," he said. Then he collected himself and pushed through the door. Sie and Raahi came cautiously after him.

The room had a dozen round tables and, at the far end, an arch over a counter where platters of breakfast items were set out for self-service, along with silver coffee and tea servers and trays of china cups. But the foods were barely recognizable, they were so old, and there were spider webs on the tarnished carafes.

That was odd enough, but what really caught their attention was the presence at many of the tables of small groups of people posed stiffly in their chairs, staring blankly, some of them also spider-webbed. They had evidently been eating breakfast: plates, cups, and bowls were arrayed before them. Some of them were holding silverware. But every one of them was facing the door, staring at a point just about where Sie was standing, their faces fixed in expressions of surprise and alarm.

Sie gasped and Raahi said, "They're not moving, are they? And why does it smell like last week's breakfast was never cleared away?"

"It wasn't," Sie said.

Master D hurried to the nearest table, where he waved his hand in front of one of the lifeless, mannequin-like people then reached out to touch a shoulder. "Stasis spell. *Very* strong. Never seen anything like it. This must be from one of those more distant worlds where magic is stronger and more heartless than ours."

"There are worlds like that?" Raahi asked, coming over to peer into the face of an immobile woman. "How horrible!"

"That's where the most frightening of our folktales come from, actually," Master D said. "The Brothers Grimm were interworld travelers who had some hair-raising escapes. I really don't know why their stories are considered suitable for young children. Huh," he added as he approached an elderly white-haired man with a neatly trimmed beard. "This is the headmaster. I'd hoped he could tell us what's going on."

"There must be a counterspell," Sie said. "Is it an immobilization? I know how to unweave those."

"They don't last long enough for dust to accumulate. This is something more powerful. Otherworld magic is hard to countermand unless you happen to know it, but you wouldn't, would you, because it's not from our world."

"You're starting to sound like your double," Sie complained.

"Am I lecturing? I fall back on it when I'm upset," Master D said. "The point is that they're unrecoverable unless we track down the otherworld sorcerer who did this."

"Do you think it's safe for *us* to be here?" Raahi asked. "Oops!" He'd brushed a man's arm and bumped a spoon out of his hand; it clattered to the floor.

"I doubt it," Master D said as he glanced around. "But here we are."

"A lecture would be more reassuring," Sie said, frowning.

"At least," Master D continued, "we're being chased by lightning, not a stasis spell. So far, we haven't been attacked by the otherworlder who did *this*."

"But we haven't actually been struck by lighting," Raahi pointed out. "Maybe they were herding us with it."

"Too complicated," Master D said. "Usually the simplest explanation is the correct one."

Raahi pulled out a chair and sat down at an empty table. "Usually," he agreed. "Okay, let's analyze this:

A. The Hunt Club identifies me as from a parallel world and tries to find out what door I'm using.

B. Rudy follows me, presumably hoping I'll lead him to the doorway. Then he chases us in the modern world.

So, *C.*, he *already* moves back and forth like us.

Then, *D.*, why does the Hunt Club need us?" He paused. "My analysis isn't going very well," he concluded with a frown.

"Perhaps," Master Dorsenhaal said, "they don't have as good a way of moving between worlds as you do. Some connections are like long tunnels or complex caves. If they're using one of those, they'll be eager to find a better one."

"Could be," Raahi said, absentmindedly reaching for a teacup and almost putting it to his lips before realizing it was caked with dry, dusty brown stains. "Yuck! Therefore, *E.*, it still could be simply a conspiracy to track down a doorway. But that doesn't explain what happened here."

"I'm suspicious," Sie said, "that they already knew about this and wanted to get us to come here. Which brings us back to Raahi's theory that the lightning was herding us. What if their real goal is to get hold of this otherworld magic? And, somehow, driving *us* here is going to help them do that."

"A potent otherworld battle magic," Master D said, sounding thoughtful. "It's certainly a strong motive for a group like the Hunt Club. But what role do *we* play? Oh!"

One of the many-paned windows burst inward, scattering glass onto an empty table beneath it. A glowing column appeared there.

The column of light in the broken window solidified into a faint, flickering image of a tall young man in a BAAM uniform with a wide face topped by stiff blond hair. His dark blue eyes were set deep beneath heavy brows. "A good question!" he said. "We figured that if the girl's side door and your closet were both in danger of compromise, you'd hurry here. Paranoia Protocol, right?" He chuckled rather meanly.

"So it's *F.* then," Raahi said with a frown. "They move freely between worlds, but they wanted us to *think* they were after our doors so we'd come here. And the whole plot was kicked off by beating me up. Right, Rudy? I'd recognize your unpleasant voice anywhere. You're one of the ones who punched me. Repeatedly, as a matter of fact."

"Fond memories," the boy said. "And I'm the one who chased you to that stupid gallery. I don't know how you slipped away from me there, but it doesn't matter. I was just supposed to add to the impression that you weren't safe in Boston." He grinned again.

"*You* beat Raahi up?" Sie took a threatening step toward him.

"Bruiser and Chauncey held him," Rudy's flickering image replied. "Thuggy and I did the punching. We need to come up with a nickname for Chauncey, don't we? He's a lot meaner than he sounds." He chuckled.

"Then you deserve *this!*" Sie raised her hands and pushed a powerful gust of wind at him.

It was so sudden and strong that it cleared the table in front of the young man, blowing several abandoned coffee cups out the broken window. But the boy's image was unaffected. "Nice wind-working," he said. "See, that's why we need you. We've been studying you. You're the best magic-worker out there, at least of school age, and I hate nerds, but *he's* the cleverest student we know. And when it comes to dealing with aliens, you can't actually be too clever, can you?" He eyed Raahi. "Our leader wanted to be sure you had the skills he needed, so he set a series of challenges to test you. Too bad you survived them! I was rooting for the snake. *And* the tree branches." He flashed that increasingly annoying grin.

"If you weren't an illusion . . ." Sie growled. "Where *are* you? Are you even in Oxford?"

"Of course not. You'd have to be crazy to be there now."

"And why is that?" Master D asked.

"You said it yourself," Rudy snapped. "This is the work of a powerful alien race. That's why we want their magic."

"Did you really call some otherworlders an 'alien race'?" Raahi demanded. "Sounds like you're planning to exploit them before you even meet them!"

"We don't care about them. We just want their magic. And that's where *you* come in. You're going to bring us one of their sorcerers so we can torture his secrets out of him. You have until sunset." He began to fade away.

"Sunset on which side of the Atlantic?" Raahi asked.

"And what happens then?" Sie added.

Rudi's flickering image grew a little stronger. "Death, of course."

"I've risked my life many times," Master D said. "As for these students, I'm afraid I can't allow them to be threatened in such an unpleasant manner. I'll be sending them away at once."

"Not *your* death, stupid," the boy said, grinning. "Theirs!" Then he faded completely away. In his place, a thin glowing line formed a circular window, and inside it, another flickering view appeared. The view was of Great Aunt Gen and Raahi's mother. They were back to back, taped to wooden chairs. Behind them stood a half dozen beefy BAAM students, two of them holding vicious-looking axes. One of them drew his hand across his neck. Then the vision faded and the broken window revealed the gray, wet morning again.

"Those *jerks!*" Sie exploded. "I'll *kill* them! Let's go back and beat the stuffing out of them *right now!*"

"Was that . . ." Raahi asked, sounding stricken.

"Yes. They have Aunt Gen *and* your maa," Silent said, "but we're going to free them!"

"I'm sorry to say," Master D said, "that it's probably not that simple."

Sie glared at him. "You're the one who said we should leave Aunt Gen and come here," she snapped. "That was a *terrible* idea! Why should I believe you now?"

"I'm sorry about that, but clearly those boys didn't cook up this scheme on their own."

"Then who's behind them?" Raahi demanded. "Because *I* think we should capture whoever's in charge, tie *them* to a chair, and beat *them* until they tell us where they're holding Maa and Aunt Gen." His expression was so grim that Sie knew he meant every word.

"Whoever the mastermind is, we can assume they've hidden both their identity and their hostages," Master D said. "Rushing back to Boston might be pointless without more information."

"Are you saying we have to do what they want?" Sie exclaimed. "Because I'm with Raahi. I think we should focus on finding the ringleader and freeing them as soon as possible! Never mind about otherworlders and their magic."

"We aren't in a position to dictate terms," Master D said with a frown. "Not yet. Our first task is to find out what happened here." He began to walk slowly around the dining room.

"But what about—" Sie began.

"Silent. Raahi." Master D turned to face them. "We have to be smart. Logical. Focused."

"Yes," Raahi said. "Focused on freeing our—"

"No. This is the center of everything. The focus of our—*your*—enemies. Please give it, shall we say, two hours?" He pulled his pocket watch out and frowned at it then slipped it back.

Sie bit her lip and Raahi tapped his foot nervously. "What do you think?" he asked.

Sie shook her head. "I don't like it. None of it! But . . . two hours." She sighed. "Since we're already here."

"Then let's find out what happened," Raahi said.

"Thank you," Master D said.

"Where is the college's door?" Sie asked.

Master D nodded. "A perceptive question," he said, "since presumably that's where the otherworlder came from. I think it's time to introduce you to the college's best kept secret: the multidoor."

TWELVE

Frozen

They left the professors immobile at their dusty breakfast and Master D led the way further into the building, winding past comfortable sitting rooms, a library, and a lecture hall, until he came to a tall unmarked door.

When opened, the door revealed a strange room, octagonal in shape, going up several stories to a ceiling made of arching glass. Rain was pelting on the glass.

They joined him in the middle of the room—which had no furniture, just an oak floor—and stood there staring. The room had eight tall doors, one on each side of the octagon. Seven of the doors looked identical, with oak panels and brass doorknobs—except that the door they had come through had a brass plaque engraved with "Linacre College" on it. The eighth door, originally like the others, was blackened around its edges as if it had been set on fire. And over most of its surface, someone had written long columns of runic characters in blue chalk.

A short stub of chalk lay on the floor by the door.

And also laying there, still as death, one hand near the chalk as if she'd held onto it until her last moment, was a woman with curly brown hair, thick wire-rimmed glasses, a tweed suit, and sensible brown leather shoes such as a professor might choose to wear while lecturing.

"Oh dear. Dear me." Master D looked close to tears. "I'm afraid it's Ursula Sontheil, Master of Otherworld Studies. She is, or *was*, a brilliant scholar, and one of my closest friends from my days here." He knelt to check her neck for a pulse then stood abruptly with a sharp intake of breath.

"What?" Sie demanded.

"She's freezing cold. I don't know what to make of it."

"Dead?" Raahi asked.

"Not yet, but she's in some sort of low temperature coma." He frowned. "This is terrible! I'm so sorry you're entangled in whatever cruel game is being played here."

"What did she write on the door?" Sie asked. "Is it a variant of ancient Sumerian?"

"Glyphs of some sort," Raahi said. "It might almost be Phoenician, but I don't know why there are circles around some of the runes."

"I assume," Master D said, "that it's an otherworld language. It's probably from wherever this door leads to."

"Where *do* these doors lead?" Sie asked.

"That's a good question. The room is built above a large octagonal stone. Hundreds of years ago, there was a garden around that stone with paths leading off in eight directions. The college was built on the site of that garden so that people would no longer wander into it and disappear. You see, the paths had a way of taking people elsewhere."

"So the doors lead to different worlds," Raahi said.

"Yes. I apologize for the lecture, but I should add that these doors lead to different worlds *at different times*. They rotate according to the cycles of the moon. In any single month, there are seven worlds to be found through them, but the next month, seven different worlds."

"Do any of them lead back to Boston?" Sie asked.

"No," Master D said, "but there's a portal in the headmaster's office that goes to London, and once there, we could sneak into a portal in Benjamin Franklin's old house. It connects to the Boston Public Library."

"I didn't know Franklin lived in London," Raahi said.

"For two years in the lead-up to the American Revolution," Master D said.

"Back to business, please?" Sie said.

"Right. The new moon is tomorrow night," Raahi pointed out. "So this door won't lead to the right world after that, but it doesn't actually matter since our deadline from the Hunt Club is tonight. I think we should assume they mean sunset in Boston since that's where they are."

"Either way, we're in a hurry," Sie said, stepping carefully around the fallen body of the professor and reaching for the knob.

"No!" Master D cried. "Don't open that door!"

"Whoever attacked the college is obviously in there," Sie said. "We need to find them and make them reverse their spell."

"Ah, Sie?" Raahi had leaned over to pick up a little notebook that was poking out of the master's coat pocket. "Hang on a sec." He was alternately flipping through the notebook and examining the runes on the door. "It looks like she went through at the beginning of the month and met someone she calls the 'Bee Woman.' They exchanged information." He flipped through several more pages. "Vocabulary, formulas for workings, and so forth." His gaze alternated between the runes on the door and the notebook. "But then someone else came through and attacked the college. Master Sontheil was in the dining room when it happened, but she'd been told about a block and she notes here that she formed the runic shape of it under the table and pretended to be caught in the stasis spell until the attacker left. Then she used what she'd learned to seal the door in order to prevent further intrusions—and just in time, judging by the burn marks. They seemed to have tried to force their way back in."

"I'm sure she did all she could," Master D said, gazing at the fallen master.

"What does *this* mark mean?" Sie asked, pointing to a rune that was repeated three times at the bottom of the left hand column.

"Uh, I saw it in here," Raahi said, flipping through the notebook. "Yes, it's for completion. It activated the working and made the rest of the runes lock the door. And pretty well, I'd say, since the otherworlders must have tried to come back by blasting their way through but couldn't."

"So," Sie said, starting to rub off the chalk of the ending runes, "if we erase these, the door will open?"

"Not so fast," Master D said. "You have no idea how to defend against their magic."

"Actually," Raahi said, "her notes include counters that seem to work like our wards. You drawn them in the air with your hands."

"If they work, why is she like this?" Master D asked.

"I don't think she was attacked," Raahi said. "She's behind a well-warded door."

"Then how did she get so cold?" Master D frowned. "The stasis spell in the dining room didn't make them cold." He paused, looking down at her. "We were in school together. She was a few years ahead and she was very kind and helpful to us younger students. May I see those wardings?" Master D added. "I should study her notes before I go in."

Raahi handed him the notebook. "Have you ever read about honey-bee 'waggle dances'?" he asked, peering at one of the circled runes on the door. "Because bees actually make similar shapes on their honey-comb to show their sisters where to find nectar." But no one answered; they were too accustomed to his obscure comments to pay attention to this one.

"Her scholarship was always top rate," Master D said as he read the notebook. "As I hoped," he added. "Here's a blocking rune. We ought to practice it. Let me see." He began to trace a shape in the air. It started with looping ovals followed by a diagonal zigzag and ending with a very rapid shaking of the index finger. "There, I think that's right," he said. "You should try it. Oh, and here's another one. She says it blocks stasis spells. It goes like . . ." He began to scribe more shapes in the air, but before he could finish, he gasped and dropped to one knee, holding his wrist. "Ow!"

Sie and Raahi hurried to help him back to his feet.

"Let me see," Sie said, taking hold of his wrist. "That's strange!" she exclaimed.

"What?" Raahi asked.

"His arm is cold."

"I feel chilled and faint," he complained. "I think I should sit."

They helped Master D to the nearest wall and eased him to a seated position.

"Their magic must be harmful for us to use," Sie said.

Master D nodded. "I suppose she knew that but used it anyway to keep them from coming back."

"I'm going to try," Raahi said, taking the notebook out of Master D's hand. "Good thing there's a glass ceiling."

"Glass? Why?" Master D asked.

"Lots of light so I can read the notes easily," Raahi said. "Okay, here goes."

"Careful, Raahi," Sie said. "It's obviously dangerous."

"They have my mother. Besides, I have a theory. Remember what Rudy said about their wanting a team of students?" He began to form shapes in the air. Soon he had finished the first rune and started the next.

"Are you getting cold?" Sie asked.

"No," he said as he finished that one. "Just a little cool. Let me try the first block again." When he'd finished, he flipped back and forth in the notebook for some time. "Apparently," he concluded, "the Bee Woman said only young people can do magic. The Bee Woman was getting too old for it. She was in her late teens."

"Are you saying," Master D said, "that the spells are safe for teenagers but not adults?"

"Right," Raahi said. "So *we'll* go through that door, and *you'll* wait here."

"I don't think that's a good—wait, it *does* suggest a motive for quite a few things," Master D said.

"Things?" Sie asked.

Master D nodded. "Some adult is probably planning to have the Hunt Club students wield the magic for them. *And* they would need teenagers with remarkable skills and courage to reopen this door. I can't think of a better choice than you two. Which means it might not be such a good idea for us to open that door," Master D continued. "No matter what leverage they have."

"Then how will we undo the stasis spell on the faculty?" Raahi demanded. "And rescue Aunt Gen and my maa?"

"I think we should study those notes more carefully first, and I could try to get in touch with the Boston Custodian and see if he knows how to reach any Custodians on this side of the—Wait, what are you doing?"

Silent had gone back to the burnt door and was rubbing out the final three runes. "I'm going in," she said. "I'll get the counter or bring someone who knows how to perform it. And then we'll trade otherworld magic for hostages. You don't actually think we're going to sit around discussing things while our loved ones are in danger, do you?" She frowned at Master D. "Do you even have a family?"

He shrugged. "It's customary for Custodians not to."

"That's stupid," Sie said. She turned to Raahi. "The notebook, please."

"I'm coming." He slipped the notebook into his back pocket. "You're going to need a scholar."

"Help me up," Master D demanded as he tried to get back to his feet. "I'll come with you."

"I think, sir," Raahi said, "that you'd better wait here until you recover your strength. We'll be back as soon as possible. However," he added, "if we don't get back by sunset, seal the door again, okay?"

"Wait!"

Thump. The door swung closed, leaving Master Dorsenhaal and the frozen professor alone in the eight-sided chamber.

Some time later, just as Master D had managed to get to his feet with one hand out to steady himself against the wall, the groundskeeper popped his head through the door leading back to the college. "Hello there!" he said, sounding jovial. "Would you care for some fish? I've had an exceptionally good catch today."

Master D turned to gape at him. "What?"

"Fish," he repeated, offering a bucket filled with them for Master D to examine. "I'll just bring them 'round to the kitchen." He went off down the corridor, whistling a jaunty tune.

"The man's losing it," Master D muttered. "Too bad, since it would be helpful if he could tell us what happened." Then he sighed and sat down again. "I better wait until I'm not quite so faint," he muttered, "before I follow Silent and Raahi. I do hope they'll be all right."

THIRTEEN

Overs and Unders

The suns were a little higher in the sky on the other side of the door.

Two suns, both smaller than the one they were accustomed to, but in combination bright enough to make them squint and shade their eyes with their hands.

They were standing in a garden. A really big garden. Not only was it big in that it stretched off to the horizon but also the flowers were huge. They looked like ordinary pansies, daisies, and so on except that they were a yard across and on thick stems that stood ten to twenty feet high.

"It's just as well we didn't wear our coats," Raahi said after a moment of taking it all in. He undid the topmost button on his shirt and rolled up his sleeves. The suns were hot, the air was warm, and there was a heavy moistness to the atmosphere. They could hear, off in the distance, the buzz of garden bees.

"Nice spot for a vacation," Sie said, "but where are the otherworlders?"

"Maybe flying overhead?" Raahi suggested as, with a deafening buzz, something big raced across the sky. "Was that a helicopter?"

"Uh, no," she said, moving closer to him. "You won't believe this, but . . ."

"An airplane? A flying saucer?"

"Actually, a giant bumblebee."

"Of course! The giant flowers. Makes sense. Do you think they're dangerous?"

"Hopefully they eat nectar, not people."

"Something's coming. I hear rustling."

"You always hear—wait, I do too." She tugged him toward a thick bush covered with giant daisies and they slipped behind its lush foliage.

Down the path came a girl. She was an inch or two shorter than Silent and looked a year or two younger. And she looked surprisingly human: Two legs. Two arms. A pleasant-looking face. Skin deeply tanned where it was exposed to the sun; then again who wouldn't be, in a world with more than one sun? Blue eyes. Long hair twisted high on top of her head—that part was not so ordinary. A "beehive" hairstyle, Sie thought it was called. Also, she wore a skirt apparently made of huge yellow petals sewn together, along with a short-sleeved shirt stitched out of giant daisy petals.

The girl stopped and stared at the door.

Peeking out from behind a giant leaf, both Sie and Raahi were struck by what an odd sight the door was. No wonder she was staring. It had an oak frame around it, just like on the other side, but this frame stood up in the middle of the garden.

"Hello!" the girl called. "Who's there? Come out where I can see you."

"She speaks English," Raahi whispered. "Is that strange?"

"Many things are strange," Sie whispered back, "but she doesn't seem dangerous. Shall we?"

Raahi nodded and they stepped out onto the path in front of the door.

The girl looked surprised. "You're like me!" she exclaimed.

"Well, I suppose we're similar, generally speaking," Raahi replied. "Although my eyes are darker in color and so is my skin and hair, and—"

"No, I mean you're not overs," she interrupted. "When I went through the door, they were overs."

"Overs?" Sie asked. "What does *that* mean?"

"Overs. You know. Over-sized. Over-aged. We don't have them here. Mistress has us hunt them, the ones that don't freeze themselves to death first. They're no use to her because they can't use her magic, and she says they're not as obedient as we are."

Raahi exchanged a glance with Sie. "We noticed that your magic seems to hurt our adults—I mean our overs."

"We don't like to talk about that."

"No, of course," Sie said, trying to sound sympathetic, "but does everyone get too old to do magic?"

"Well . . . eventually," she admitted. "*You* know. We, uh, over and out." The girl frowned.

"Anyway, here we are!" Sie said, trying to lift the mood. "I'm Silent, and this is Raahi. Pleased to meet you! We're, um, visiting. What an interesting place! Are all the gardens this big?"

The girl cocked her head at them again. An eyebrow rose.

Sie gestured around them. "Giant flowers everywhere?"

"That's just how it is. Everywhere is garden to support the bees. And the bees support us. See?" She pulled something out of a pocket in her bright yellow skirt. It looked like a round rice cake. "They feed us honey-cakes. And sometimes we slice up earthworms." She made a circle with her arms; apparently worms were much larger there too. "We call it wormsteak. I saw *your* food. It looked yucky."

"You went to the dining hall at the college?" Sie asked.

She shrugged. "I don't know those words, but I think so. Overs sitting around with dark stinky drinks in their cups. And, uh, dry greasy cakes. No honey in them."

"Tea and toast," Raahi said. "So you *were* there. Did you see who did that to them?"

"The overs? Me, of course. Stopped them. It was my directs. From Mistress."

"You were following directions?" Sie frowned.

"Of course! You too, right?" She reached up and touched the back of her neck, feeling something there.

"Your rune-markings," Raahi said before Silent could ask her about her neck. "They look like diagrams of the waggle dances of honeybees. Do you keep bees for their honey like we do? Is that one now?"

Another heavy shape went buzzing overhead. It was so loud that they had to wait for it to pass before they could talk again.

"No, the other way round. We're kept by Mistress," the girl explained. "Our queen. We do her directs and we sleep in empty cells in her hive. Don't you?"

Sie and Raahi exchanged a *very* surprised look.

"Not really," Sie said. "I like honey though." She tried another smile.

"Did you come to take it?" The girl frowned. "I will have to report you."

"You misunderstand. We keep hives of our own and have all the honey we need. We just wanted to meet you," Sie said.

"I still have to report to Mistress. She did not think unders lived in that world because I didn't see any. And when I told her it was rainy and hardly any sun, she decided she was not interested. She said get rid of anyone who knows about us and wait for the door to change. But now, you."

"Do you explore a different world each month?" Sie asked.

The girl nodded.

"What does your mistress direct you to do when you find a world that's sunny?" Raahi asked.

"We clear the path."

"Clear the path of *what*?" Raahi asked.

"Anyone who might bother the bees. And then some of our bees stay to set up a new hive."

"How?" Sie asked.

"A princess builds a hive in the new world and starts a colony there. And when the door comes back around, Mistress talks to her daughters to see how things are going."

"How nice," Raahi said. "One big happy family."

"And sometimes they fight."

"Fight? Why?" Raahi looked surprised.

"If the princess is strong, she might try to come back and kill Mistress and take over here."

"Kill her mother?" Sie exclaimed.

"That's how bees are. So when the door comes around again, we scout the new colony, and if there's too big a hive, Mistress sneaks in and kills them. Then she sends a new princess and starts over again."

"Sounds pointless," Raahi said.

"And violent," Sie added. "I'm glad she didn't like our world."

"Yes, but now that we know there are unders like you to work for a colony, Mistress might change her mind." The girl smiled again.

"Wait, did you already report us?" Raahi demanded.

She touched the back of her neck. "Have to. No secrets."

"What's on your neck?" Sie asked, stepping closer to her.

"Bee fuzz," the girl said. "Don't you have it?"

"May I see?" Sie asked, flashing a winning smile.

The girl shrugged but allowed Sie to come up close enough to glance at the back of her neck.

"It looks like the yellow and black fur on a bumblebee," Sie said. "There's a patch of it. How did you get that?"

"We're nipped at birth. See, sometimes a girl has a baby before she over and outs. Then the bees take it to their nursery and keep it until it can work."

"Do the bees speak English?" Raahi asked, frowning. (He was trying to imagine how babies raised by giant bees could learn to speak.)

"You mean our undertalk? The bees spell it into us before we leave the nursery. I don't know how. They've been visiting otherworlds for a long time and when they don't fight with the otherworld queen, they trade."

"Trade what? Magic?" Sie glanced at Raahi.

"You talk too much. Now we go to your world again to see how many unders are there for working." She headed up the path toward the door.

"Uh, just a minute," Raahi said, reaching out and grasping her by the arm.

She pulled away easily. Raahi was surprised by her strength. Facing him, she raised her hand and began tracing something in the air.

"The block!" Sie shouted, hurrying to carve her own ward-rune in the air.

Raahi raised his hand, but before he could start, there was a *pop* and a strong smell of wildflower honey. And then he was not moving; he had been caught by the girl's stasis spell.

She turned toward Sie and formed the shape in the air again. There was another *pop.*

Sie glared at her. "Take it off him."

"Why aren't you . . ."

"Take it off him now!" Sie repeated angrily.

"How did you know the block?"

"I know a lot of magic," Sie growled. "Do you know how to block *my* magic?"

The girl stiffened. "I'm not sure. Why?"

Silent raised her hands and sent a blast of air at the girl.

It threw her onto her rear. "Hey! That hurt!"

"I'm just getting started. Now take the stasis off him!"

"I will report this," the girl said, getting a bit unsteadily to her feet.

"Or not." Sie waved her hands again.

This time the wind came in a tight spiral, spinning and lifting both the bee girl and the frozen Raahi. With a tilt of her hand, Sie made the whirlwind move up the path toward the door.

The door slapped open and the whirlwind tumbled them through.

FOURTEEN

Bee Fuzz

Raahi was deposited with a thump in the middle of the floor, one hand raised, a frown on his face, still immobile. The bee girl tumbled in after him, stumbling, but jumped to her feet to face Master D, who was still sitting against the wall. She began to form a rune with her hand, but Sie, who had rushed in after her, grabbed her arm and spun her around. "Don't even think about it," she hissed.

"But he's an over!" the girl objected, shaking free of Sie's grasp. "My direct is to kill all of them. But if Mistress isn't paying attention, I let them run away into the wild areas," she added with a frown. "Because someday it will be me."

"Well, now you have new directions," Sie said. "If you don't want to find out what else I can do, keep your hands at your sides. Understand?"

"Sorry, but I only follow directs from Mistress," the girl said. "I wish I didn't have to, but . . ." She raised her hand again.

There was a tremendous *bang.* It was as if the air had converged from either side and clapped like giant hands. In fact, it had. Sie had slapped her hands together and the air had followed her lead. The bee girl, mouth half open, eyes rolling upward, collapsed in the middle of the floor, her head landing on Raahi's immobile sneakers.

Master D worked his way to his feet, adjusted his wire-rimmed glasses, pulled out his pocket watch, frowned at it, gave it a shake, frowned at it again, then let it fall so that it swung on the end of its chain. "I take it," he said, "that this is one of the otherworlders? Her attire is rather floral. Was she about to use a stasis spell on me?"

"Or worse."

"I don't suppose she mentioned the antidote?"

"Not yet. She takes commands from a giant queen bee." Sie knelt down and pointed out the black and yellow patch of bee fuzz. "She says this is her link to the bees."

"Hmm." Master D looked down, using Sie's shoulder for support. "I'm still a bit dizzy, I'm afraid, but isn't this interesting?" He got down on his knees and felt it carefully, then reached into a side pocket and took out a pocketknife. Opening it, he began to poke around the edges of the patch.

The girl's eyelids fluttered and she moaned.

Master D muttered a medical spell in ancient Greek. Sie thought it was to ease the pain. Then he gritted his teeth and, with a quick movement, sliced the patch away.

The girl's neck was instantly covered in blood. She moaned again.

"Oh dear," he said. "It seems to have been anchored rather deeply. Probably into her nervous system and, via the spine, up to her brain." He added more Greek. Sie recognized a staunching and something intended to mend or heal wounds. She had taken magical first aid at school, but this was more advanced.

The bee girl stopped moaning and sat up, blinking. "What did you do to me?" she demanded.

"The question, I should think, is what did the *bees* do to you?" Master D said.

She felt her neck, then, alarm spreading across her face, felt it again. "Hey! Where is my hive!" Tears sprang to her eyes. "You cut me away from my hive!" Then she burst out sobbing and collapsed on the floor with her face in her hands. It was both moving and oddly theatrical.

"Oh dear," Master D said.

"Let's step out into the hall," Sie suggested. "We need to talk."

Leaving the immobile Raahi, the frozen professor, and the sobbing girl in the eight-sided room, they went a few yards down the hall to where it was quieter. "The kids work for giant bees," Sie said. "And there aren't any adults. They call them 'overs' and they 'over and out' them."

Master D's eyebrow shot up. "Unfortunate. But the girl speaks English. It makes you wonder."

"If Raahi weren't stasis-spelled, he'd be happy to delve into an academic discussion," Sie said, "but *I'm* more interested in how we're going to make things right. For starters, we need to force her to tell us how to undo her stasis."

"Y-es," Master D said, "but it *is* interesting, isn't it?"

"What's interesting?" Sie asked.

"She speaks the King's English, as they say, suggesting she might have ancestors from here."

"Where, Oxford?"

He nodded. "The door rotates, after all. It's possible the bees kidnapped children to work for them in the distant past."

Sie shrugged. "I know you're a professor and like to think about things, but time's wasting. What should we *do* with her?"

"I'm getting to that," Master D said. "You see, there is a hard and fast rule that you don't, you *can't*, just take people from their world and force them to come to ours. Not even to save your own family members. As a Custodian, I'm sworn to uphold the rules. I would have to stop you if you tried to break them."

"I doubt you could," Sie said.

"But if her ancestors were stolen from here, then it *is* allowed to bring her into our world, assuming she wants to be rescued. When you talk to her, point out that she'll have a much longer and freer life here, out of reach of the queen bee."

"I will help you," the bee girl said. She was standing in the doorway, listening to them. "If you help my sisters too."

"Your sisters?" Sie repeated. "Uh, how many sisters do you have?" (She was recalling that bee colonies are made up mostly of female worker bees that are, technically, all sisters.)

"Two. We're not like bees," she added, guessing what Sie was thinking. "Actually, most of us don't have any siblings at all."

"And that would be," Master D said, polishing his glasses, "because of the artificially shortened life spans, I presume?"

The bee girl gave him a stern look. "Because nobody lives long enough to give birth more than once, yes."

"Sorry. I can see how it might be a sore point," he said.

"Are all overs this annoying?" the girl asked.

"Most of them, yes, but you'll love my Aunt Generous. *If* we manage to save her," Sie added with a frown. "So, you have two sisters and you want to bring them here?"

"We're identical triplets. They're probably worried about me."

"Will they notice you're gone?" Sie asked.

"They have already. I can't feel them, which means they can't feel me." She reached up and felt the back of her neck. "The hive connects us to the Mistress and her directing, but it also connects us to each other, even through that door. By the way, I'm April," she added with a tentative smile.

Sie reached out to shake her hand, but April did not respond. "Oh, you don't shake?"

"Hands? No, we bow our heads like bees do." April bent her head to the left side of Sie's face. "Touching antennae, see?"

"Except you don't have antennae," Sie pointed out.

"We're an inferior race. That's what they tell us. No antennae, wings, or stingers. So we have to work for them."

"Simply because you don't have antennae?" Sie asked, incredulous.

"Consider," Master D said, "Dr. Martin Luther King's observation that discrimination of a people makes sure 'the lie of their inferiority is accepted as truth in the society dominating them.' We shall have to educate her in the ways of oppression."

"Yes but maybe not by lecturing her?" Sie suggested.

"Fair point," Master D said. "April, would you be willing to take that stasis spell off Raahi? He might," Master D added when April looked uncertain, "be helpful in freeing your sisters."

April eyed him uncertainly, then her face lit up with a smile. "You're right!" she announced. "Come on." And then she pushed through the door into the eight-sided room again, where Raahi was still standing frozen in the middle. "We don't usually undo our work," she said, "but when I was being trained they showed us how—just in case we spelled another explorer by mistake." She turned to Raahi and made a complex series of gestures with her hands. (Sie watched carefully as she worked.)

Raahi sucked in a quick breath, then his eyes opened wide in surprise. "How did I get here?" he demanded. "And why is *she* here?"

"You missed a few developments," Sie said. "Welcome back." She gave him a quick hug, which he seemed to find embarrassing. "Next time, do the warding faster," Sie added. "She got you with a stasis and I lifted you both here. Now she's on our side and we're going to rescue her sisters."

"We are?" He blinked. "Are you sure that's wise?"

Silent shrugged. "I'm just making this up as I go along, but I think they'll be helpful."

"If you say so." Raahi turned and, without hesitation, pushed through the chalk-marked door again.

"I like him," April said. "Sorry I immobilized him, but it was my directs."

"I know," Sie said. "Come on. Oh, and Master D? Why don't you stay and guard the door."

"Now see here, I really can't allow you to—"

"You're an over," April interrupted. "Everyone will try to kill you."

"Well . . ."

"We've got this," Sie said. And then they went through the door and into the hot suns of the other world again.

FIFTEEN

Ali Sleeps In

Ali had a good night's sleep. So good, in fact, that she slept late and barely had time to grab a cinnamon bun from her kitchen as she rushed out the door.

Her hurried walk to GALA took her along the north side of Boston Common and past the pond with the swan boats. The boats were all docked at that hour of the morning as Ali hurried to turn the corner at the bottom of the park and go down Commonwealth Ave.

With just a few blocks until she reached the corner where her school stood, she slowed her pace to take a bite of the bun.

A black carriage with its shades down kept pace with her as she walked, but she did not think anything of it. There were quite a few carriages and carts on the busy road. But when the carriage door swung open and two large boys in BAAM uniforms jumped out, she paused to stare.

When they rushed up to her, grinning in an oddly unfriendly manner, she dropped the half-eaten bun and her eyes grew wide. "Uh, what do you want?" she demanded.

"We're giving you a ride," one of the boys said as they grabbed her.

"Hey!" she shouted as they started to drag her toward the carriage.

SIXTEEN

Bee-sieged

In the bee world, Silent, Raahi, and April stepped into an even hotter and sunnier landscape. The suns were higher and the air was thick with the perfume of giant flowers. "Much better!" April said. "I don't like how cold your world is. If I move there, I'm going to need warmer clothes."

"Where are your sisters?" Sie asked.

April shrugged. "Probably weeding. Or turning over compost piles. They garden all day. I'm unusual. I'm assigned to exploring. It's because I'm a natural."

"At exploring?" Sie asked.

"I'm good at magic and I can go through the door every day and not get sick, like you." (Sie and Raahi didn't think to ask her how she knew that they were betweeners.) "My sisters are talented, too, but the Mistress says they'll only go exploring if I don't come back. Keeping some of the talented ones back is smart. Mistress is like that."

"Because sometimes explorers don't return?" Raahi asked.

"Of course. You never know what you'll meet on the other side of the door. Come on." She headed off down the stone pathway, and Sie and Raahi, with a nervous exchange of glances, followed.

They wound through overarching flowers until they turned a corner and the path led beneath sunflower plants as tall as trees, their gigantic flowers spreading out eighty feet above ground. Around stems as thick as tree trunks, dozen of children and younger teens were raking the soil. High above them, they could hear the buzzing of gigantic bees.

Sie and Raahi hesitated.

"Come on," April said. "My sisters are up ahead."

Raahi frowned. It seemed strange to him that April was so certain about where her sisters were when she had just told them that her connection was gone, but he followed Silent, who was keeping pace with April.

"What about the bees?" Sie asked. "Will they bother us?"

April glanced upward. "Only the Mistress listens. The others gather nectar. I see my sisters," she added, taking off at a jog.

"Where did she go?" Raahi asked—he'd lost sight of her.

"Up ahead. She's with two more girls *just* like her," Sie said. "And now they're coming this way."

The girl in the lead, presumably April, was grinning, but the other two were frowning. "This is May and June," April said when she reached them. "They don't really understand what's going on, but I asked them to come to the door with me."

"Let's go," Raahi said, turning and leading the way up the stone path.

"Hi," Sie said. "I'm Silent."

"Not very," one of the triplets said and exchanged a look with the other.

"Uh, right. Shall we?" Sie turned and followed Raahi.

"We can't go there," the third triplet, June, said. "Mistress doesn't allow anyone but explorers to go to the door."

"No, June, they're trying to help us," April said. "You don't have to do the directs. Come on, I'll show you."

"Sister," May said. "We love you, but you know we can't go against a direct. Sorry." And then she raised her hand and began to mark runes in the air.

Sie and Raahi rushed to form ward-runes.

"June, help me!" May cried. And then June began her own runic gestures, so that Sie and Raahi had to form more wards.

The duel went on for several rounds with May and June taking turns attacking while Sie, Raahi, and April cast counters. It might have gone on that way for quite some time if it weren't for one of the worker bees.

The queen bee must have sent it directions of its own, because it dove downward, weaving through the massive heart-shaped leaves. As it approached, the buzz of its wings rose to a roar.

The bee was nearly at them, its watermelon-sized eyes glittering with reflected sunlight off a thousand mirrored facets, when Sie shouted, *"Dormeo!"*

The bee landed beside them. Folding its legs beneath its massive body and letting its antennas droop, it laid its head down on the path.

"What did you do to her?" June demanded. "Is she dead?"

"Sound asleep," Sie snapped. "Want to join it?"

May and June exchanged a surprised look then turned and raised their hands as if about to send some especially nasty magic Sie's way. But before they could, Sie called out another command: *"Parere me!"*

May and June stopped, mouths open and eyes vacant. And then, as if being manipulated by invisible puppet strings, they lowered their arms jerkily and began to walk stiff-legged toward the bee. "And don't interfere," Sie snapped, directing her words at April. "I won't hurt them, but I certainly won't let them hurt us!"

"What did you do to my sisters?" April demanded. They were standing stiffly beside the sleeping bee.

"They're fine. They're just hypnotized and waiting for instructions," Sie said.

"Wow," Raahi exclaimed. "That's impressive, Sie, but I thought it was strictly forbidden to use magic to hypnotize anyone."

"It is."

"Let them go!" April demanded. "I won't have you giving my sisters their directs. It's not nice to do that to people!"

"Tell that to your queen bee," Sie said. "Now, here's the plan. You are going to do what I say, April, or else I'll hypnotize you too. We need to get to the door before more worker bees come, so climb up onto that bee. *Please.*"

April frowned. "We're not allowed to ride them."

"Exigent circumstances," Sie snapped.

"What does that mean?" April asked.

"It means," Raahi offered, "that you better hurry up because I hear more bees coming."

At that, April scrambled onto the fuzzy back of the bee and reached down to help her hypnotized sisters, who, at Sie's mental command, had begun to climb stiffly up after her. Then Sie was pushing Raahi up and climbing after him. "Grab some bee fur!" she shouted as the bee's wings began to beat the air on either side of them. And then it was rising up and swooping over the gardeners, who screamed and dropped their rakes and hoes.

As they straddled the bee's back and gripped the black and yellow fur, Sie closed her eyes and pushed her instructions into its mind. The bee was surprisingly compliant—nothing like the fierce owl she'd communicated with so recently. Their flight leveled off and the bee made a sweeping turn toward the direction of the door.

Then something went wrong.

SEVENTEEN

Late

"Let go of me!" Ali screamed, struggling to free herself from the young men who still had her by her arms.

A woman in a long dress was hurrying toward them, her shopping basket over one arm. "Leave the young person alone!" she cried, hitting one of the boys with her basket, which spilled potatoes all over the cobblestone sidewalk.

"See here," an elderly man with thick whiskers exclaimed, stopping in front of them. "That's not very gentlemanly, is it?"

"Buzz off," one of the boys snarled.

"You asked for it," the elderly man said, swinging his walking stick at the boys' legs.

Snap. The woman and the man stopped. Their eyes rolled up and their eyelids fluttered, then they collapsed to the sidewalk, unconscious. Someone had struck them with a powerful working. Ali wondered who. *Probably some creep hiding in the carriage,* she thought, redoubling her efforts to pull free.

The boys had dragged her to the carriage door, and one was trying to pull her in while the other pushed her, when there was a *pop* and another man appeared. He was thin, slightly stooped, and dressed in a brown tweed suit. He had a large book under one arm and gold-rimmed glasses halfway down his nose.

He blinked at the scene in front of him. Then he frowned and opened the book.

"Help!" Ali cried. "They're kidnapping me!"

"Yes, I see. And if I may take the liberty . . ." He was leafing through the pages of his book. "Ah, here we are." And then, to Ali's annoyance, he started reading out loud. It was something obscure, not even in English.

"Hey!" she cried as one of her feet slipped and she started to fall into the carriage.

BANG. This time the sound was much louder, nearly deafening her. She fell hard, expecting to land inside the carriage. Instead, she fell into the elegantly tiled entry hall of her school.

Her headmistress was standing there, looking down at her. "You're late, Ali," she said. "I was just about to close the gate. *And* you ought to know by now that you're not supposed to use magic outside these doors!"

"I, I didn't, ma'am," Ali said, struggling to her feet.

"That was obviously a full blown transport. And since when do you know how to transport yourself? You're lucky all of you came along. Most people leave body parts behind when they try. Here, let me help you straighten up before you go to class."

"It was some man in gold glasses with a big book."

"Hmm. Sounds like the local Custodian. But why?"

"I was being kidnapped."

"Kidnapped? Really." The headmistress did not seem to believe her.

"By two students from BAAM. They were trying to pull me into their carriage!"

"Were they? And what exactly did they say?" Her tone was still doubtful.

"Um, they said they were going to give me a ride." Ali realized it did not sound nearly as serious as it was. "But they were *not* being nice!"

"My guess is that the boys from BAAM, who were obviously running late themselves, *and* the Custodian, who must have just been passing by, were trying to help you make up for lost time. Did you sleep late?"

"Well, yes, but—"

"There!" the headmistress said, straightening Ali's collar. "Now, I believe you have a Theory of Workings lecture to attend. We mustn't neglect our Three W's: workings, weavings, and wards."

And so Ali was hurried off to class, still wondering who had rescued her so abruptly and why anyone would want to kidnap her in the first place. *At least Sie takes the same class,* she thought, *so I can tell her what happened.*

She saved a seat for Silent, who had not yet arrived.

When the instructor cleared her throat and the room quieted, Ali began to get seriously worried. Her best friend was never late.

EIGHTEEN

Stung

The bee dropped downward then swooped violently up as if trying to buck them off its back. It felt to Sie like some other intelligence was taking control. Some mind that was similarly odd and insect-like but far stronger and more determined to resist. *Oh no!* Sie thought. *That must be the queen!*

Sie pushed hard, trying to overcome the queen's influence and take control of the bee again. There was a strange mental tug of war, each of them struggling to gain the upper hand but unable to. The bee, confused, flew in erratic zigzags, and they had to hunch down and grip the fur tightly to stay on.

Then another firm thought came into the fight. Someone else was pushing their thoughts into the worker bee's mind. Pushing alongside Sie and against the queen.

The queen bee was pushed out and Sie's new ally whispered the thought, *You control the bee. I'll guard against the queen.*

It's Raahi, Sie thought, surprised. *And in the nick of time!* And then she focused on the bee and its flight, bringing it back around and aiming it in the direction of the door.

"More bees coming," April warned.

Soon they could hear the buzzing of strong wings approaching from behind. April leaned forward to wrap her arms protectively around her sisters, who were sitting very straight and staring calmly ahead as if they had no awareness that they were careening through the sky on the back of a gigantic bee.

The bee they were riding was so weighted down that it flew slower than the bees giving chase. The buzz of their wings rose to a roar and Raahi leaned forward and shouted to Sie, "Can we hypnotize them?"

Sie wondered about that. It was taking a lot of effort to maintain the link with the bee they were riding. "Too many balls," she called back to Raahi.

"In the air? Like juggling?" Raahi asked.

"Yes, but . . ." An idea had occurred to her. She thought it might be possible to push just one single, strong command into their minds and to do it so quickly that the queen would not have a chance to block her. Struggling to calm herself, she tried to think of something clever. Some simple, clear order that would be like an endless loop they had to follow. *A loop,* she thought. *Why don't I make them fly in a circle!*

"*Cingi ad sinistram!*" she called out in a ringing voice at the same time she pushed the thought into the bees' minds. It meant "circle to the left."

"They're turning," Raahi said. "Good work! Wait, they've looped around and they're coming back toward us. No, it's okay—they're circling away again. In fact they seem to be flying around and around."

"Exactly. But I doubt it will last very long, so . . ." Sie aimed the bee they were riding toward the door and brought it to a hard landing on the path. "Hurry!" she exclaimed as she slid down the side.

Soon they were on the path beside the bee, which she had put back to sleep.

April was clinging to her sisters. "Can we free them now?" she asked.

"Not yet." Sie pointed toward the door and May and June began to walk mechanically toward it, forcing April to walk between them in order to keep a grip on their arms.

Raahi had hurried ahead of them and was struggling with the knob, but he seemed unable to turn it. "We may have a problem," he said. "The door's locked. And darn it! The queen is getting past my block." The sleeping bee began to twitch and buzz its wings.

April circled her hands in a furious rune. As Raahi dove to the side, fire leapt from her and rushed at the door.

"Uh, April?" he said as he got to his feet and straightened his glasses. "What makes you think that's going to work any better this time?"

"It's how they trained us to get through locked doors," she said with a shrug.

"We use a simpler approach in our world," Sie snapped, waving a hand to extinguish the fire. "It's called knocking." And then she rapped on the door. "Master Dorsenhaal," she called. "Open up!"

The door cracked open and Master D peaked out. "Oh! Sorry about that. There was so much buzzing that I thought the bees were attacking."

"They were," Sie said as she pushed past him, waved the others in, slammed the door, and knelt down to chalk the closing runes once again. "There!" she said, standing and brushing the chalk off her hands. "And I'm taking my hypnosis off your sisters, April, so please try to keep them under— darn!"

May and June had leapt into action and started to form runes, but Sie muttered something and they stopped, their arms falling limply. "They'll have to stay under hypnosis," Sie said. "Sorry abut that. We can lift it once we disconnect them from the hive."

April frowned. "That isn't nice," she said. "I hate to see them that way."

"It's only temporary," Raahi pointed out.

"No, it's not!" April exclaimed. "If it's like stasis, it lasts until, uh . . ." She bit her lip.

"Wait, does stasis kill people?" Raahi demanded.

April nodded.

"It's a way to 'out' people, isn't it?" Raahi pressed. "Unless you take it off them. Right?"

April looked down.

"Then let's take it off the faculty and staff of Linacre College," Raahi said. "Now."

"What about the freezing?" Silent asked. "Master Sontheil's as cold as ice." She gestured toward the immobile form on the floor.

"I didn't do that," April exclaimed. "It's her fault for using bee magic."

"And does that 'out' people too?" Raahi asked.

April raised an eyebrow. "Maybe. Do you like her even though she's an over?"

"We don't even know her," Sie said, "but we still want to save her. We don't go around killing overs," she explained. "Or *anyone.*"

"That's good!" April exclaimed. "I wish Mistress felt that way." She knelt down next to Master Sontheil. "Freezing's the worst. It kills you faster than stasis." She held her hands over the frozen master. "I'm not supposed to thaw them unless they have information Mistress wants, but do you want me to try?"

Master D gave April a stern look as he said, "Thaw her at once."

"I wasn't talking to that over," April complained, addressing Sie and Raahi.

"We'd really like it if you thawed her out," Sie said. "Could you back up and give her room to work, Master D?"

April smiled. "For you, sure thing!" Her hands formed figure eights in the air above Master Sontheil and she muttered something buzzy. Then she reached to feel Master Sontheil's wrist. She looked worried. "I don't think it worked." There was a long pause. "I'm sorry," April said, getting to her feet.

Master D took off his glasses and cleaned them with a very wrinkled handkerchief. They seemed to have gotten wet.

"Wait!" Raahi exclaimed. "I just heard her breathe!"

And then Master Sontheil took a deep breath and began breathing evenly.

"Is she all right?" Raahi asked as Master D knelt beside her.

"I think so," he said. "Her pulse is almost normal now and she's a lot warmer. Thank you, April. Thank you very much."

"I'm glad she's not dead," April said. "Now can you let my sisters go?"

"Wait a second," Raahi said. "There's something going on outside the door."

"Something?" Sie repeated. "Like what?"

"Buzzing and scratching. Like bees are trying to get in." He went over and pressed his ear to the door.

Master Sontheil's eyes opened, and she tried to sit up but was unable to. She groaned.

"Ursula, are you all right?" Master D exclaimed.

"That's the girl . . ." She whispered, pointing a shaky finger at April. "Stop her!"

"She's on our side now," Sie said.

Master D nodded. "Things have progressed since you were frozen, Ursula. Rest and recover, and I'll explain soon."

"Uh, guys?" It was Raahi, listening intently. "I think there are a bunch of bees outside the door."

"The wards should hold," Master D said, frowning. "I think."

"Watch out!" It was April, shouting as she dove and knocked Raahi away from the door so that they fell in a heap.

And then, before anyone could react, there was a tremendous splintering and something sharp and very lethal penetrated the door, piercing the air precisely where Raahi had just been standing. *It was a gigantic stinger.*

"Th-thanks," Raahi stuttered as he disentangled himself and got shakily to his feet. "How did you know that was going to happen?"

April jumped up, brushing the petals of her skirt into place. "Strengthen the door!" she cried. "I can't. My magic doesn't work against Mistress. Ow!" She leaned over, wincing and holding her head in her hands.

"Did you bump your head?" Raahi asked. "Oh!" he added in surprise as the stinger—which was shiny purple-black and about two feet long—slipped back out of the door, leaving a bright jagged hole.

April, still holding her head, turned to Silent. "Girl, do something!"

"Wood seems an inadequate choice in hindsight," Master D said, studying the hole in the door. "I presume they didn't anticipate an attack by gigantic bees when they built this room."

"Stand behind me, everyone," Sie said. "This might be hard to control." She closed her eyes, took a deep, steadying breath, then as the others waited in suspense, whispered, *"Nunc evocant deam antiquis, Ninkasi, et eius magi regina, Kubaba."*

The light flickered and the floor shook under them. Master D gasped and Raahi's eyes opened wide. "Are you certain it's a good idea to evoke ancient Sumerian magic?" Raahi asked.

Silent ignored him and waited until the vibrations in the floor stopped and the light steadied. Then she raised her hands and cried, *"Vertunt ferro!"*

The light winked out completely—not only in the room but above the building through the skylights. It looked like night. The only illumination was the thin spear of sunlight bursting through the hole the stinger had made. There was a tense moment in which they could hear each others' nervous breathing and nothing else. Then the quiet was rent by a metallic grinding that finally ended with a shuddering *crraaack*.

The light flooded into the room from above. Everything was back to how it had been. Everything except the door, which, although it still had blue chalk marks, was no longer wood. It was a thick slab of iron.

Silent sat down heavily.

"Are you all right?" Raahi asked, hurrying over to her.

"That took a lot of effort."

"A large-scale alchemical transformation by voice command alone," Master D said, frowning. "Without the use of a catalyst. It's considered nearly impossible! And were you invoking the goddess Ninkasi and her sorceress Kubaba, Queen of ancient Sumeria?" He was staring at Silent in apparent disbelief.

"Lots of things were invented in ancient Sumeria," Raahi pointed out. "The wheel. Writing. Poetry. Beer. And more to the point, sorcery."

"I know," Master D said, "but Sumerian sorcery is so terribly powerful and poorly understood that no one, I mean *no one,* uses it today. I don't know what you were thinking, Silent. I'll have to tell Generous about this!"

"Do you need medical attention, Sie?" Raahi asked.

Sie shook her head. "But give me a hand up." April and Raahi hurried to pull her to a standing position. "I'll be all right," she added. "I'm glad that worked."

April smiled. "I like your world's magic," she said. "You'll have to teach me."

"After you teach us how to remove the stasis," Sie said.

"Yes, April," Master D said. "I must insist that you take your stasis off the masters in the dining hall."

April frowned. "He's an over. Why does he keep giving me directs?"

"Directions? Well, overs tend to do that," Sie replied. "It's a bad habit they have, but it *would* be good to free the others."

"My sisters first," April said.

"I'll remove their connections from the hive," Master D said. "Then Sie can free them."

"Now the over wants to bargain," April complained.

"What if we take care of your sisters first, then we go to the dining hall?" Raahi asked.

April smiled. "Since it's you who's asking," she said. "But *I* cut off their patches."

"Master D knows medical magic," Sie said. "Will you let him help?"

"As long as I hold the tool. What tool did you use?" she demanded, turning toward him.

"A pocketknife," he said. "Here." He hinged open the steel blade and muttered something over it.

"What was that?" April demanded.

"A disinfectant so the blade will be clean."

"Oh. Give it to me."

And then, in a very matter-of-fact way, April sliced the bee fur patches off both of her sisters' necks while Master D spoke his staunching and healing spells. "They won't be happy," she said when she was done. "I wasn't."

"It must be quite a change," Sie said. "Is it nice not being controlled?"

"I like it, but I have an independent streak. That's why they send me through the door. Mistress says I have more initiative than most."

"Your sisters don't have as much initiative?" Raahi asked.

April shrugged. "Not so much. I'll have to tell them what to do now."

"Well, perhaps you could tell them not to cast stasis spells," Master D said.

"Since you asked nicely," April said.

"I've taken my hypnosis off them," Sie announced.

"Let's step back," Master D suggested, "and leave this to April to sort out."

Surprise and alarm flashed across May and June's faces. They began to shout at April. A great many "What did the over do to us?" and "Why can't we feel the others anymore?" filled the room as they waved their arms and generally got more and more excited until Raahi finally put his fingers to his mouth and made such a loud whistle that everyone turned toward him.

NINETEEN

Making Plans

"You should be happy," Raahi admonished. "Your sister freed you from the Mistress's control and you don't have to work for the bees anymore. So please stop arguing and let's get to work. We have to rescue a lot of people!"

April, May, and June put their heads close together and began to whisper. After a while, April seemed to win them over. She turned to Raahi and said, "We'll help you, but you have to find us a new hive to sleep in and new flowers to care for. That's all my sisters know. They don't feel right unless they're gardening."

"I think," Master D said, "that the masters of Linacre College would be pleased to offer you room and board in exchange for help with the gardens. Shall we revive them and see if they're agreeable to the terms?"

More whispering with April, and then, to their great relief, nods from April's sisters. But they did not know how to undo stasis spells, so April told them to wait in the octagonal room with the recovering professor, who had closed her eyes and seemed to be asleep.

"Please keep an eye on her and come find us if she wakes up and needs anything," Sie said, and they nodded again.

They had recovered from the initial shock of being disconnected from their hive and were talking about what they might do now that they didn't have to take directions from the queen. (Eat as much honey as they liked, sleep late, plant the flowers *they* liked best, etc.)

"You'll be nice to the over?" Sie asked, looking over her shoulder as she left the room, and they smiled and nodded.

Master D led the way to the dining hall, where April demonstrated the runic hand motions to undo the stasis and then April, Raahi, and Sie circulated, weaving shapes with their hands in front of the afflicted. Master D hurried from one to another of the masters, explaining what had happened and trying to calm them down because they were waking up highly agitated, many of them knocking over their chairs as they leapt out of them and some of them shouting cries of alarm.

One master spat out a dry piece of toast he'd been eating when the stasis took hold. Another master tried to take a sip of tea but finding it dried up and dusty, she dropped the cup in surprise. The headmaster, a short man with a neat white beard and thick glasses, woke up sputtering mad and cast a weaving of his own that caught April and lifted her off the floor. It was an air-weaving that pinned her to the ceiling until Sie came over and took it off while Master D tried to calm him down.

When everyone, including the cooks back in the kitchen area, were reanimated, Raahi found an empty water glass and *dinged* it with a fork until the dining hall fell quiet. "Excuse me," he said, "I know you've just suffered a traumatic experience, but we still have to rescue our loved ones and it would be helpful to know who's behind this malfeasance. Does anyone have information that might be of assistance?"

Sie gave him a look. His wording sounded exceptionally nerdy, even for him, but of course he wasn't used to an audience of Oxford masters.

The room fell quiet for a moment as the masters listened to Raahi's question, then it became even louder than before. Everyone had a theory, being academics. After a while, Sie herded Raahi and April out of the room. "They're not going to be any help at all," she said. "And Master D seems to be just as eager to argue as the rest of them."

"Let's see if Master Sontheil has revived enough to talk to us," Raahi suggested.

April's sisters were sitting together on the floor in the hallway outside the multidoor room, heads together, whispering. "The over woke up," they reported before going back to their private conversation.

Inside the octagonal room, the master was sitting with her back against the wall.

"How are you feeling?" Sie asked.

"I'm rather weak, but honestly, I never expected to live through the experience, so I'm very grateful for that. Have you been working on them in the dining hall?"

"Yes," Sie said. "They seem fine. Argumentative, though."

"Good! That means they've returned to normal," she said. "I don't suppose you could run back there and get me a cup of tea? It might be reviving."

"Nothing's ready," Sie said. "The cooks are still recovering. But if you don't think it would be against the rules, I could magic you up a cup."

"Exigent circumstances, I think. Please do your best."

"I could transport a pot of tea from, uh—are there any good places in town?"

"The Grand Cafe on High Street, my dear. A pot of the Lady Grey, please, and why don't you fetch me some smoked salmon and cream cheese finger sandwiches while you're at it? I feel as if I haven't eaten in days."

"You haven't," Raahi pointed out.

Sie had learned (in Terrain and Brain, a course she'd taken last semester) to enter a light trance and scan surrounding areas magically. However, even though she cast her vision up and down the street twice over, there was no Grand Cafe. "Are you sure it's on High Street?" she asked.

"Well, not in this world, sorry. I forgot to mention that it's a modern-day tea shop."

"We're in the side door world," Sie pointed out. "High Street is full of horses and wagons."

"Look for the Angel Inn and Hotel. It's the same building. We turned its entrance into a portal. You just have to whisper Grand Cafe as you cross the threshold. Reverse the effect by saying Angel Inn on the way out. It's such a nice little convenience to those of us who enjoy popping into the modern world to pick up specialty items we can't get now."

"That's against every rule, I bet," Raahi said. "They'd never allow it in Boston."

"Hasn't Augie Dorsenhaal ever taken you out for Boston cream pie at the Parker House?" she asked. "No? You must ask him to when this is over." She smiled.

"Pie?" Raahi repeated. "Why?"

"Well, the Parker House Hotel in Boston has the most amazing French chef—and one of the hotel suites has a door that's actually a portal. I've used it to go for dessert there." She smiled.

"Not to distract us even more," Raahi said, "but are you saying that people cross the Atlantic Ocean just to get dessert?"

"Not *just* for pie. The author Charles Dickens rents that suite," the master said. "I think he enjoys being able to pop back home to London when he's working in Boston, but don't tell anyone. The portal's unlicensed."

"I detect a casualness about portals that might explain how this whole mess was possible in the first place," Raahi complained. "But you may as well go ahead, Sie, and get her the tea. I don't see how it could make things any worse."

"All right." Silent, returning to her trance, entered the hotel and muttered the spell. She found herself looking into a neat, modern cafe. Passing through the seating area, she peered into the kitchen and identified an order that was about to be picked up by a waitress. It seemed to include what Master Sontheil wanted. There were scones and little tea cakes, too, but Sie was feeling hungry and didn't see any harm in bringing extra. So she wove the transport, whisking the big serving platter away just before the waitress got to it. Her expression was priceless.

There was a shimmering and the tray appeared on the wooden floor in front of Master Sontheil. The room immediately filled with appetizing smells.

"It's Earl Grey, not Lady Grey, but I'm impressed," the master said, reaching over to pour herself a cup. "Where did you learn that?"

"My Aunt Gen. We magic things from the kitchen to the dining room for fun. She says it's good practice."

"You're Generous Lee's girl? She was one of the most gifted students ever to go through here. Her name is on every award plaque. I don't suppose you paid for any of this, by the way?"

"I'm her niece. And I don't have any money. Sorry."

"I'll stop by and explain next time I'm there. Ah, that's much better!" she added after a sip. "Now, why don't you update me."

"Did you see the attack on the school?" Sie asked.

"I did, and I'm afraid it happened because of me. You see, I study otherworlds as they cycle through these doors. Usually I just go a few yards in and write notes. In this instance, I met a woman in her late teens who said she was hiding. She asked me how I'd lived so long."

"We're supposed to out the overs," April explained. "But *I* let them run away. It's tricky to do it without Mistress knowing, so I 'miss' when I shoot my rune-spells at them."

"She must have been one of yours, then. We got to talking and we shared quite a bit of information about our worlds. She was very interested in our concealments. In return, she told me about bee magic."

Raahi produced her notebook from his pocket. "This was very helpful," he said as he handed it back to her.

"Thank you. Unfortunately, I found I couldn't use bee magic myself without feeling ill. Nor could the young woman who told me about it. Too old, she said."

"Mistress realized you were talking to someone," April added, "and wanted to punish you. She also wanted to see if she liked your world. So she sent me. I am—I *was*—her explorer."

"You're the one who attacked us. I recognize you," Master Sontheil said.

April nodded. "Sorry, but it was a direct. An order. I was supposed to kill anyone who saw me, but Mistress lets me decide what rune to use, so I put them in stasis. I hoped you'd be able to undo it before it was too late."

"And now you've undone the harm you caused. Thank you. But why are there two more of you?" Master Sontheil waved toward May and June, who, curious, had come in and were standing behind April.

"My sisters. They'll do as I say. What do you want us to do? Is there a garden we can tend?"

"The groundskeeper will no doubt appreciate your help. He's become quite vague in his old age and spends most of his time fishing."

"We'll get right to work," April said. "Unless there's anything else you need?" She glanced at Sie and Raahi.

"As a matter of fact, yes," Raahi said. "Sie, can you explain?"

Sie frowned. "We think some adult associated with Raahi's school is using a gang of students to try to get hold of your world's magic. They've kidnapped Raahi's mother and my aunt, and they're demanding we bring them someone who can teach them your magic."

"Oh dear!" Master Sontheil exclaimed.

"You want to trade *me* for *them*?" April asked, looking alarmed.

"No, of course not," Sie said. "But maybe we could teach them a few runes or something?"

"I wouldn't do that," Master Sontheil said. "And I wouldn't trust them to give up their prisoners. They don't sound trustworthy."

"Then we're no better off than before," Sie said, discouraged.

"We shall trick them," April said.

"How?" Sie asked.

"I don't know, but the boy will think of something. He's full of ideas." She waved a hand in Raahi's direction.

"Will he?" Sie asked, looking at him.

"I'm thinking," Raahi said. "For starters, what do we know that they don't? That's how you trick someone. You have to know something they don't."

"They seem to know a lot," Sie complained. "They're the ones who knew about bee magic in the first place."

Master Sontheil frowned. "Now, how did that little secret get out? I'm always very discreet about my work. Although I do discuss it with my colleagues in the dining hall, so . . ."

"So *someone* here is a spy," Sie said. "Don't say anything else to your colleagues, please."

"No, I'd better not. Ah, here's Augie."

Master D came into the room. "It took a while to sort things out with the headmaster," he said. "How are you, Ursula?"

"Much better," Master Sontheil said. "Want a sandwich?"

"Don't mind if I do," Master D said. "Any progress on our plans? I presume that's what you've been talking ab—"

"Triplets!" Raahi exclaimed.

"Yes, they do look remarkably alike," Master D agreed. "I suppose you haven't had a clear look at them until now?"

"That's what no one else could possibly know. No one's seen her sisters! Please close the door, Master D."

"All right, but do explain."

"I can't," Raahi continued. "I haven't figured it out yet. But there must be *some* way to take advantage of it."

"Of what? That there are three of them?" Master D asked.

"Yes. We could pretend we're trading one of them for the hostages. And then . . . do you know how to disappear, April?"

"Of course. It's part of explorer training." She held up one hand and gestured toward it with the other and it flickered and faded from sight. "Like that?" She waved her other hand and it flickered back.

"Uh, wow. Right." Raahi seemed startled. "Uh, can you go through walls too?"

"Difficult," April said. "You'd have to use a live transit spell for that."

"Which is what, exactly?" Raahi asked.

"Here, I'll show you," she said. "May, you'll have to open a landing place for me."

May and April positioned themselves on opposite sides of the room and began to carve shapes in the air.

With a loud *pop*, April disappeared.

May's movements became more frantic. "I'm not strong enough!" she cried. "June, help me!"

June hurried to her sister's side and began forming shapes too. The shimmering grew brighter, and then, with another *pop*, April appeared in front of them.

"About time," she complained after several deep breaths. "There's no air in the in-between."

"That was incredible!" Master Sontheil said, scribbling in her notebook.

"Don't bother writing it down," April said. "It doesn't work unless you have someone just like you to draw you to the other end. There are certain spells only twins or triplets can do. See, worker bees are all identical sisters, so that's part of their magic."

Raahi smiled. "Unique triplet magic. We'll trick them with it. April, you can pretend we're trading you, but once we get my mother and Sie's aunt back, your sisters can bring *you* back."

"It's hard unless you're close," April said. "And what if they hurt me first?"

"I think that's a lot to ask of her," Master D said.

"It's okay," May said. They turned and stared at her. "We don't need to trick them. We'll just beat them."

"Beat them?" Raahi repeated, looking puzzled. "How?"

"We'll all go. All three. We can stasis-spell everyone," May said.

"She's right," April said. "It's simple!"

Sie shook her head. "I don't think they'll accept three of you," she said. "It would be risky for them. They only need one to teach them the spells."

"They won't know," April said. "We'll merge."

"Merge?" Sie repeated. "What do you mean?"

"Watch," April said. "Sisters?"

They held hands. They began to spin. Bright yellow petals rose up from their skirts. They spun so fast, they were a blur. And then they stopped, except now there was just one of them. "See?" she said.

"Wait, where are your sisters?" Sie asked.

"Inside," April said. "Try to pick me up. Really! Just try."

Sie wrapped her arms around April—but was unable to lift her. "You're way too heavy!"

"Three in one, see?" April said. "Bees do it to sneak into an enemy's hive. Then they separate and start to fight. It's really exciting."

"That's the plan, then," Raahi said. "We'll attack them with the same bee magic they want to steal. Seems fitting! Would you like to separate now?" he added.

April began to twirl like a dancer. When she came out of her spin, her sisters twirled out. "Good trick, right?" one of them asked. (Sie thought it was June.)

"Very good," Raahi agreed, "but we mustn't let *anyone* see all three of you or word might get back to our enemies."

"I told you the boy would think of something," April said with a grin in Raahi's direction. "We like him!"

And so it was decided that April and her sisters would spin themselves together once again and then they'd all go to the dining room and try to reach the Hunt Club.

TWENTY

What Next?

After the Custodian from the Boston Public Library transported Ali to her school, he examined the two pedestrians who had been rendered unconscious. "Good! Only minor injuries," he said to himself. He leaned over to speak a few first aid chants, then he brought them back to consciousness and helped them to their feet. "Thank you for assisting," he said. "I'm sorry you were inconvenienced. Now, if you'd care to go on about your morning's business, I'll take care of the miscreants." He glanced meaningfully at the dark carriage, and the pedestrians hurried off.

He straightened his glasses, opened his book, read from it, and tucked it firmly back under his arm. Then he stood there waiting. He assumed whoever was in the carriage would come out; he had immobilized their horses.

He liked horses. All animals, really. So he was sorry to have turned the horses to stone. Permanently. Nothing in his world's magic could undo the working. He would have preferred a more temporary measure, but there seemed to be a powerful sorcerer behind the current mischief, which meant drastic measures were needed.

The carriage door opened and the boys from BAAM got out again. "Hey!" one of them complained. "Why'd you do that?"

"By *that*, young man," the Custodian said, "do you refer to rescuing the young woman, reviving the pedestrians, or disabling the horses?"

"All three." It was a firm, decisive voice with a hint of a crisp French accent. It was coming from the dark interior of the carriage. "Boys, see what you can do about him."

The students grinned eagerly. They looked excited.

The Custodian raised an eyebrow and studied them through his gold-rimmed glasses. "Are you absolutely certain you want to duel?" he asked. Then he stood there, book under his arm, blinking in the morning sunlight as the two students from BAAM approached him.

One of the young men raised a wind that picked up a bench from the nearby park and blew it over Arlington Street and above Commonwealth Ave. The other screwed the lid off a large mason jar and threw the contents, a steaming acid, at him. (Presumably the acid had been made even more potent via alchemy—not a nice thing to toss at anyone!)

Things stopped. Certain things. The boys. The liquid—it was mid-splash, suspended in the air. The bench, which was about ten feet up and tumbling downward when it froze. While the boys continued to be frozen, the liquid unsplashed back into the jar, the lid twisted into place, and the bench tumbled backward until it landed in the park again. Then the jar itself, with its acid, disappeared with a *pop*. (The Custodian had sent it to a lockbox he maintained in his office, which was somewhere in the Boston Public Library's vast and winding basement.)

Then the Custodian let the boys go free.

They cursed and ran toward him.

Giving them a vaguely disapproving look, he muttered something and they popped out of sight, just like Ali and the jar of acid had.

"Where did you send them?" A hollow-cheeked, white-bearded face and broad shoulders had appeared. A man had opened the blind and was looking out the carriage window.

"To school, of course. They're late. Do I know you?"

"You ruined my horses."

"Yes. I didn't want you galloping off."

"It's inexcusable! You Custodians are *always* meddling in other people's business. Such a bad habit!"

"About your hostages. Where are you holding them?" the Custodian demanded.

"We can discuss that in a minute," Saint-Omer said, "but first, let's get reacquainted. You are Haratin Draconis, otherwise known as Harold. I've bumped into you before."

"The Egypt breach? Of course. You look considerably older though." The Custodian frowned. "What are you doing here in Boston? I thought we'd locked you up."

"I'm the dueling master at BAAM now, but it took me years to escape."

"You got what you deserved. You were stealing otherworld magic to use in taking over our world," the Custodian pointed out. "Not to mention that you'd captured and tortured a member of a CRACK team of roving Custodians."

"Ah well. I was young and foolish back then."

"Just tell me where you're holding the hostages."

"What's it to you? I mean, really! Why do you even care?"

"It's my job," the Custodian said. "And . . ." He paused, frowning.

"Does Generous Lee mean something to you? Is she, perhaps, special?"

"That is not the point." The Custodian pulled his book out from under his arm and opened it.

Before he could find the page he was looking for, Master Saint-Omer stepped out of the carriage. He was carrying a small wooden chest under one arm. "Just a minute. Perhaps we can work things out." He smiled. "Your name literally means 'Dragon of the Haratins,'" he continued. "As a boy in Morocco, you became famous for transforming into a dragon to defend your people. It therefore seems especially fitting to offer this little artifact to you." He opened the chest and tossed a large metal ring at the Custodian's feet. It was about a foot in diameter and finely wrought in the form of a dragon chasing its own tail.

The Custodian peered at it. It appeared to be made of platinum. "Otherworld?" he asked.

"I brought it through on the trip before the one you so rudely interrupted," Saint-Omer said.

"Chasing its own tail. A so-called strange loop." The Custodian frowned. "Are you turning it in?"

"Yes. I'm hoping it might induce you to leave me alone this time," Saint-Omer said. "And perhaps I'll release the hostages too. It might be pleasant to put more nefarious activities behind me and spend the school year actually teaching. I find I enjoy working with the boys."

The Custodian studied him. "It's hard to believe that you're suddenly eager to change your stripes, but . . ." He shrugged. "At least it's a good start to turn in your otherworld artifacts. What exactly does this one do?" He leaned over and reached for the dragon ring.

"You'll see," Master Saint-Omer said with a satisfied smile as the Custodian's hand closed around it.

The sun flickered as the Custodian touched the ring.

His glasses slipped down his nose and shattered on the cobblestones and the book slipped from beneath his arm and thumped to the sidewalk. A frown creased his forehead. He began to mutter counters, wards, and blocks.

They did not seem to do any good. The dragon ring was expanding at an exponential rate. Soon it was so large that Saint-Omer hurried to get back inside his carriage and lock the door.

The dragon had come to life. Its forked tongue darted in and out of its gigantic fanged mouth and its platinum eyes flashed beneath heavy metal brows. It looped rapidly around the Custodian, squeezing him.

Farther down the sidewalk, someone screamed.

TWENTY-ONE

The Unexpected

All was quiet and peaceful in the dining hall. The empty tables shone with fresh wax. Chairs had been pushed in neatly. A panel had been rolled down to close the serving counter.

"After being trapped here, everyone was eager to move on," Master D explained. "And the cooks wanted to go home."

"We aren't here for food," Sie said. "We're here to talk to that jerk again. Hey!" she called, facing the broken window in which he'd appeared before. "Are you there?"

A flash of lighting and a rumble from the heavy clouds outside the window reminded them that the weather was still stormy. However, no one shimmered into view to speak with them.

"Answer me!" Sie demanded.

Still nothing.

April came up. "You want me to get those boys for you?"

"Can you?" Sie asked.

"If they left traces, I can backtrack."

"Please," Silent said.

April made wavy signs in the air and spoke something buzzy. A bright pinpoint of light appeared. She gestured to widen it.

Pop. A middle-aged man with a military buzz cut and very dark glasses appeared in the dining room, blocking their view of the broken window and the opening April was making. He snapped his fingers and the opening closed. "That's *quite* enough," he said with a hint of a French accent.

"Who are *you?*" Raahi demanded, startled.

"The newest master here at this college." He gestured toward the floor at their feet.

"Ow!" Raahi cried. His feet were embedded in the wooden floorboards up to his ankles. Silent, April, and Master D struggled beside him, all of them trapped.

Master D spoke a warding, Sie pushed a strong wind toward the man, and April began to weave a stasis spell.

The man clapped and they all cried out in pain. He'd slapped their hands with a wind so strong that they could not complete their workings. "Let me introduce myself more fully," he said with an unpleasant grin. "I am Saccard Saint-Omer."

"Are we supposed to recognize the name?" Sie demanded. "Because your fame has not preceded you!"

"*I* know that name," Master D said with a frown. "I helped capture you and your older brother in Egypt years ago for the illegal importation of platinum magic."

The man's grin became wider. "Actually, wasn't it *we* who captured *you?*"

"That was only the opening chapter," Master D said. "What are you doing here?"

"When my brother and I escaped," he said, "we both obtained teaching posts. I came here to Oxford. Of course, I knew the bee aliens were going to attack, so I stayed off campus for that rather interesting event. I suppose you're wondering where my brother is?"

"Dueling master at BAAM," Raahi said with a frown.

"Precisely."

"And so we've found the spy," Master D said.

"And for that, you will die," the man replied. "My brother had other plans for you, but since you've delivered the alien to me here, I'll just bring it back to Boston myself." He smiled and raised both hands.

"Did you just call me 'it'?" April exclaimed, looking annoyed.

TWENTY-TWO

Gone

The dragon's long, platinum-scaled body scraped over the cobblestones as it circled the Custodian, who, having exhausted his supply of wards and workings, raised his arms above his head, closed his eyes, and shouted fierce words in some unfamiliar language, the result of which was that he burst up and into the shape of a steely blue dragon, heavily scaled from horned head to long tail.

The dragons leapt upon each other, tumbling and scraping and hissing until the nearby trees had been stripped of bark and cobblestones were turned over and tossed everywhere.

And then the platinum dragon freed itself from the grip of the blue dragon for long enough to whip around and sink its fangs into the blue dragon's tail.

With a roar, the blue dragon did the same, reaching around to bite the platinum dragon's tail.

And there they froze. The strange loop having been completed again, the peculiar magic of the otherworld artifact was to make living flesh into cold metal.

They began to shrink.

Master Saint-Omer stepped out of his carriage, which had several deep scrapes on its side, having been so near the battle. He waved a hand to repair the damage then leaned over and picked up the ring. It now consisted of *two* finely wrought metal dragons chasing each other's tails: one platinum, the other steel.

Master Saint-Omer wore a silk glove on the hand that touched the ring, and he carefully inserted the ring in a silk drawstring bag, which he placed inside the chest, which he secured by spinning the numbers of a brass combination lock on the latch. He stowed the chest in the carriage then came out with a platinum vial. Going up to the stone horses, he popped the stopper from the vial and shook a few drops of liquid on their heads. "It's a good thing I have otherworld magic," he said, "or I'd have to purchase more horses."

The stone transformation took a minute or two to reverse. At first only their heads came back to life. They flicked their ears and whickered nervously as their necks and bodies, and finally their legs and tails, came alive.

By then, Master Saint-Omer was back inside his carriage.

The horses were in harness, of course, but there was no one on the bench in the front of the carriage where a driver would normally sit. Still, the horses followed Master Saint-Omer's directions somehow; perhaps it was another piece of otherworld magic.

As the carriage picked up speed and forced a Model T to the side of the road, a driver appeared on the front bench with a shimmer. A long whip appeared in his hand with another shimmer. Master Saint-Omer was resetting his illusions so as not to be too conspicuous, although as his carriage careened down Commonwealth Ave., a great many people stared at it anyway, and those who had to swerve to avoid being hit cursed and shook their fists.

TWENTY-THREE

Bee Magic

In the dining room at Linacre College, Saccard Saint-Omer, the new master of Egyptian Studies, was just raising his hands to perform some deadly working while Silent, Raahi, April, and Master D struggled helplessly to extract themselves from the encasement spell that held their feet in the floor.

Everyone was struggling but Silent, actually. She was standing calmly, her eyes half closed, whispering a working of her own.

A large iron lamp from the front entry suddenly appeared above Saccard Saint-Omer's head and dropped on him.

The junior master lay flat on the floor, unconscious.

Silent waved at the floor and their feet were free again. "What a jerk!" she snapped.

"Did *you* do all that?" Raahi asked.

"Of course. I would've dealt with him sooner, but I wanted to hear what he had to say."

"Thank you," Master D said. "That was most helpful."

"I was also waiting to see if *you'd* deal with him," Sie said, frowning at Master D.

"Oh, well, I was still formulating my tactics," he said. "But I appreciate your stepping in."

"He's a bad over, right?" April asked.

Raahi nodded.

April gestured toward Saint-Omer and, with a sucking sound, he was pulled through another bright point of light.

"Where did you send him?" Master D exclaimed.

"I don't know. Some unfriendly world without a doorway," she said. "We're trained to do that when we don't want to kill someone but we can't have them around to attack us again."

"You opened a borehole?" Master D sounded impressed.

"If that's what you call it," April said with a shrug. "It's just a worm in time and space that wriggles around until it finds some faraway world. Do you want me to open the window to your Hunt Club now?"

"Please," Master D said. "And perhaps when this is all over, I could interview you about your methods. Very interesting from an academic point of view!"

"Overs sure are strange," April said as she worked the air in front of her with hand gestures again.

A bright circle appeared. It shone like reflective glass. Then it turned see-through and they were looking into an oval opening at a cluttered study where a mahogany desk with chipped legs sat in front of tall book-cases. April's view was not shimmery and faint like Rudy's had been; it was crisp and clear.

They stared into the room, puzzled. No one was there.

Correction. No one was there at first, but as they watched, a tall thin man with a white beard hurried in and sat down heavily on his desk chair. "Boys!" he shouted. "Get in here!"

And then the view filled with members of the Hunt Club hurrying in to sit or stand in front of the desk.

"They're at my school!" Raahi exclaimed. "That must be Saint-Omer's study!"

The boys spun around, surprised, and the man behind the desk leapt up and shouted, "I told you not to let them see me!"

"*We* didn't open a view," someone complained. "*They* did."

"You must've left traces, you idiots! You know what that means."

"We'll have to kill them?" another boy offered.

"They can hear us!" the man snapped.

"I see we have your attention," Raahi said. "Are our loved ones there?"

"Not likely, loser!" spat Rudy, the boy who had spoken to them earlier. "Did you get the alien magic?"

Raahi held up a notebook. (Master Sontheil had leant it back to him.) "This has a professor's notes about her visits to their world."

"*We* could've stolen notes," Rudy said. "That's no big deal. We want to interrogate an alien!"

"That would be me," April said, stepping forward. "I'm the one who put the faculty of Linacre College under a stasis. Except the groundskeeper. We like gardeners, so I just muddled his memory—which wasn't very hard since he was so vague to start with. Can you believe anyone could get that over, I mean old? Impressive if you think about it." She smiled.

"About time!" Rudy snapped. "Bring her to where we're keeping the hostages at—"

"Rudy," Master Saint-Omer interrupted. "Don't tell them where we're holding the hostages! They might try to free them without giving us the alien first."

"Good point, sir. Where should I tell them to meet us?"

"Don't tell them anything until they're in Boston. You can leave instructions in chalk on the sidewalk in front of that gallery. Now, would you *please* close that window!"

"Oh, and it was such a pleasure to meet your brother," April added with a mischievous smile.

Rudy began to rub out the opening, but Master Saint-Omer held up a hand to stop him. "What about my brother?" he demanded. "Where is he?"

"See you in Boston," April said and snapped her fingers. The magical window disappeared.

"Are you sure it's wise to taunt them?" Raahi asked.

"*They* weren't wise to kidnap your loved ones," April said.

"We've got to get back to Boston," Sie said, waving her hand absent-mindedly at the broken window, which reassembled itself in a rapid blur of motion.

"But not," Master D said, "through the headmaster's transatlantic portal. Too bad, because it's the only way to get there now that my closet is out of commission."

"Why can't we use the headmaster's door?" Sie asked.

"Because that way leads, eventually, to the landing of the central staircase at the Boston Public Library," Master D said with a frown.

"That's perfect," Sie said. "Let's go."

"The library door, well, actually a pair of heavy wooden doors, are—" Raahi began.

Sie cut him off. "No need for a lecture."

"I just wanted to say," Raahi said, "that the doors are described in the textbooks you lent me, so they must be well known in magical circles. We should assume the Hunt Club is watching them."

"No doubt they'll try to kill us as we emerge," Master D added, "and capture April. Of course they'll eventually try to kill us no matter *how* we travel, but let's not make it easy for them. It reminds me of when Hannibal ambushed the Roman army at—"

"Would you mind," Sie interjected, "turning your massive brains to the question of *how to get back to Boston*?"

Raahi frowned. "I think we should go out for tea."

"Tea?" Sie glared at him. "Now?"

"Can we please unfold?" April interrupted. "My sisters say it's getting stuffy."

"No one's here to see," Master D pointed out.

With a quick spin, April blurred and then firmed up again in triplicate. "That's better!" she announced. Then, her happy expression going serious, she turned to Raahi. "You're really *very* wonderful," she said. (Sie was horrified to see that she actually batted her eyelids.) "We like you a lot, boy!" At that, she took his hand in hers. "May I?"

"Uh, may you what?" Raahi looked alarmed.

"All *three* of us like you, actually," April continued, pulling him toward her. "Come on, sisters, let's show him our gratitude."

June took Raahi's other hand and May wrapped an arm around his waist from behind.

Raahi squirmed. "There's really no need to thank me!" he complained as he tried to free himself from their flowery embrace.

"We want to let you know how happy we are, all *three* of us, that we met you," April said. "And that you're trusting us to help you rescue your mother," she added. "So very sweet. Like honey! Ready, sisters?"

They nodded.

April cleared her throat and tightened her grip on his hand. Looking him in the eye, she announced in a loud voice, "We can't wait . . ." She stopped mid-sentence.

May picked up the thread. "To help you," she said.

June hurried to add, "And we can't . . ."

It was April's turn again. "Believe you trust . . ."

May wrapped up the sentence with "All of us."

"Uh, yes, but if you could just let go of—" Raahi started to say.

"Without those patches," June cut in.

"That we were . . ." April hurried to add.

"Wearing, we're not . . ." May chimed in.

"Slaves, for real!" June finished.

Then they all leaned in and kissed him on the cheeks so that he blushed and blinked his eyes rapidly behind his thick glasses. As soon as he was released, he hurried to polish the glasses on a tail of his blue Oxford shirt, studying the lenses carefully and avoiding eye contact with Sie, who was trying very hard not to laugh.

"Well," Master D said, "isn't that, ah, nice! A bit odd but no doubt from the heart. Hearts. Now, *if* you're ready, girls?"

June (or it might have been May) stepped forward and, clearing her throat, began to speak: "We three *just* wanted to *be* clear and *careful* to say, *because* you're not *enemies,* and we *are* to go *everywhere* with you." She flashed a smile and smoothed her bright yellow flower-petal skirt then stepped behind April.

"That didn't even make sense," Sie pointed out.

April smiled. "Of course it did! Now we shall go out for your English tea. I want honey in mine. *Lots* of honey."

"We're not getting tea, but we *are* going to Master Sontheil's favorite tea shop," Raahi said. "It's got a portal."

"Right!" Sie said. "Good thinking! Let's go."

"It's only set up for local use," Master D complained. "I doubt very much—"

"*I* want tea," April interrupted.

"Nobody's getting tea until we finish the rescue," Sie snapped. "Let's go!"

TWENTY-FOUR

Ali's Misadventure

Ali was concerned by Sie's absence from school. That, combined with her own near escape on the way to school, had her so on edge that she decided to sneak out during lunch and look for Sie. However, the front gate of the school was locked. And before Ali could attempt an opening chant, the headmistress appeared in the lobby and said, "Is something wrong, dear?"

Ali's attempt to explain her concerns did not impress the headmistress, who sent her off to her next class. But instead of going all the way there, she snuck down the back stairs to the kitchen pantry, where there was a rear door.

The door was wide open and a man was bringing in a wooden crate full of melons. Ali waited until he passed, then slipped outside.

Ignoring a surprised exclamation from a woman who was sitting in the driver's seat of an open wagon full of crates of vegetables, Ali rushed around the back of the school and out a narrow alley onto Commonwealth Ave. She was free.

She headed straight to Silent's house, wishing she wasn't in her school uniform—several adults gave her surprised looks as she passed them on the sidewalk, since school was obviously not out yet. When she got to Sie's house, she stopped outside, wondering what to do next.

The curtains were drawn, which seemed unusual for the middle of the day. Frowning, she slipped through the gate and went around to the side door, which was, she was startled to see, ajar. "Sie? Are you there? Miss Lee?" No one answered.

She decided to let herself in.

A short while later she was hurrying back outside and onto the sidewalk, a worried frown on her normally cheerful face and an odd instrument in her hand. She was staring at it so intently that she almost ran into a woman pushing a baby carriage.

What had she found inside Sie's house? First, she'd been surprised to see that the front parlor was in a terrible state. Chairs were knocked over, there was a rip in the couch, feathers from the seat cushions were puffed all over the room, and vases and lamps were broken. There had obviously been a struggle. Most likely a magical struggle, Ali concluded, based on the strange burns in multiple colors on the wallpaper. *Workings hurled every which way,* she decided. *But by whom?*

She'd gone through the rest of the house but found no further clues. However, Aunt Gen's little second floor library and office proved interesting. There was a tall glass case full of magical instruments of various sorts—locked, but Ali made quick work of that with an opening spell. It's true that the glass shattered into thousands of bits and fell all over the nice carpet, but at least the door opened.

Last year at GALA she'd taken Magical Instruments: Design and Handling, so she recognized many of the tools in the case. The one she took was called a tracker, and it consisted of a dial mounted on top of a small box. Beneath the dial's glass, a brass needle spun. There was also a tiny drawer on one side of the box, where you were supposed to put something closely associated with the person you wished to track.

Ali grabbed a pair of Aunt Gen's reading glasses and tried to shove them into the drawer, but they were too big to fit. Then she picked up a quill pen that was sitting on the desk. It too was oversized, but Ali snapped it in half and forced the base of it into the drawer.

The needle leapt to life. "It's working," Ali muttered. She hurried out of the house.

The tracker led her up Newbury Street to Emmanuel Church.

Ali stood on the sidewalk studying the building, which was closed for construction, and wondered what to do next.

Two young men wearing BAAM blazers elbowed rudely past her and hurried up the walk. Ignoring the "Closed" sign, they pushed through the door and slammed it behind them.

She waited until the sidewalk around her was empty, then she performed a weaving. It was a concealment designed to make her temporarily invisible by bending the light to pass around her.

She was not completely sure whether it was just coincidence that a bed of daisies disappeared, leaving a hole beside the path. Sometimes, she had to admit, odd things happened when she did magic. However, the concealment seemed to be working. Holding up a hand, she was pleased to see only a faint shimmer.

She went up the walk to the front entry, but there she paused. Pushing open a heavy oak door whose hinges squealed—she knew that from when the boys had gone in—did not seem wise. She decided to walk around the building and look for a rear entrance.

The needle went wild when she got to the south side. She was standing beneath a high stained glass window with a red cross in it.

The needle of the tracker was pointing emphatically at the stone wall of the church. It vibrated with eagerness. She decided she must be very close to Sie's aunt. But how to get inside?

Ali placed a hand on the church wall. "I wonder if I can open a door in it?" she asked out loud. She knew how to do the working in theory, but it was tricky. If not properly focused, it might bring the entire wall down. She was just getting up the courage to try when someone tapped her on the shoulder.

She spun around, realizing with regret that while concentrating on how to get through the wall, she'd let her concealment slip.

The boys she'd seen earlier were standing there, grinning. One of them was holding a roll of green tape. The other was pointing a spray can at her. *Pshshshshsh.*

"Hey, that's getting in my eyes! Cut it out!" But he didn't. Angered, she raised her hands and pushed a strong wind at them.

Nothing happened.

She tried again, shouting the words of the weaving as loud as she could. Still nothing.

"Alien tech," the boy with the spray can said as he capped it. "Works every time."

"What did you do?" Ali demanded.

"Killed your magic. Hands."

"What?"

"Hands! Put them behind your back. We're going to tape them together, stupid!"

TWENTY-FIVE

Through the Portal

"Reprogram the door," Sie said, "to take us to the Parker House Hotel." They were standing outside the Angel Inn and Hotel on Main Street in Oxford. Sie's words were directed at Master D.

"Now, see here, young woman," he said. "What gives you the impression I can just snap my fingers and make this doorway take us wherever you want?"

"Because you're a trained Custodian *and* the master of our Parallel Worlds class," she replied, eyeing him coolly. "I'm sure you know how."

"Well, it's tricky. If I make a mistake, even a small one, we might pop out anywhere or anywhen, and who knows if there will be a way back?"

"Then don't make a mistake," Sie said.

He sighed. "I'll see what I can do." Placing a hand on the doorframe, he closed his eyes and began to mumble.

"Is it Latin?" Raahi asked.

"Sounds like it," Sie said.

He opened one eye. "If you could *not* interrupt?"

They backed away.

"All right," Master D concluded, "All I need do is state our destination, uh, *ad nos hospitia* 'Parker House'— Oh dear!" he exclaimed as a heavy-set man in a fancy frock coat and a high hat hurried toward the hotel's front door.

"Excuse me, sir," Sie said, trying to detain him, but he shook her off and with an "Out of my way, street urchin," and charged through the door.

There was a clap of thunder from the gray mass of clouds overhead and a flash of bright light in the doorway. When they blinked to clear their eyes, the man was gone.

"Dear me!" Master D said. "I hope he likes Boston. Hurry now. I only set it for one minute." And then he rushed through the door to the sound of more thunder and another bright flash of light.

"You English are so very odd," April said, sounding amused.

"*We're* American," Sie pointed out. "Come on." And then they all were jogging up the steps and pushing through the door more or less at once. There was a brief view of a comfortable-looking, modest-sized lobby. Then there was such a bright flash of light that they gasped and stumbled.

It seemed oddly difficult to find anything solid to stand on. Yet they weren't falling. They floated in foggy brightness and then, just when they thought they *really* needed a proper gulp of air, the floor firmed up beneath them and they found themselves stepping into a different room. It was a large, comfortably furnished hotel suite and they had emerged in the entry to it, as if they had just stepped through the firmly closed door behind them.

A man with a sandy beard and mustache and gold-rimmed reading glasses looked up from his writing desk. "He went that way," he said, pointing toward the door behind them. "He seemed quite confused, so I told him to go down to the lobby and speak to the manager. No, I do *not* have time to talk. You're interrupting my writing!" And then he bent over his work, frowning and muttering, "Now, where *was* I before they appeared so rudely as if they were ghosts determined to haunt me . . . Ghosts . . . Good idea! One could be the Ghost of Christmas Past . . ." And then he began to scribble away, ignoring them.

"Excuse us, sir," Sie apologized as Master D hurried to open the door and wave them into the corridor.

They found themselves standing on a richly patterned carpet just outside a door marked with the numbers "138 and 139" (it was a double suite).

"Americans are *very* odd!" April proclaimed, and May and June giggled.

"*He* was English," Raahi said. "A well-known author. I suppose that's why he rented this room."

"To help us?" June asked (it have been May).

"No, to be able to give talks on both sides of the Atlantic. If you look at his schedule, you'll see that Mr. Dickens seemed to be everywhere almost at once. Biographers think he got some of his dates wrong in his diaries, but *I* think he—"

"Raahi!" Sie interrupted.

"Sorry. To Vose Galleries, to examine the sidewalk?"

"Yes, and as soon as possible," Sie agreed, "but I don't think our guests should be seen in public like that."

"Our petals are getting wilted," April complained.

"And we're cold," May added (or was it June?).

"There's a dress shop around the corner," Sie said.

"I'm not sure we have time to go shopping," Master D pointed out.

"I'll take care of it remotely," Sie said, smiling. "What size are you, April?"

April shrugged.

"I think you're a size smaller than me. Let me just . . ." She closed her eyes and entered a trance once more. She was seeing the inside of the clothing store—and selecting items she wished to "purchase."

"In the hallway of a hotel?" Raahi objected. "Really?"

"I think," Master D said, "that the guests are downstairs in the dining hall partaking of lunch, so—Oh!"

He had been interrupted by a loud *swoosh* as four whiteboard dress boxes flopped down onto the carpet, shimmering oddly. Once they had settled into their new location, Sie opened a box and offered the dress to April. It was a smart blue-and-white plaid, knee length, with long sleeves, a white lace collar, and a belted waist. In the box were also a pair of high button-up brown boots and some blue knit stockings. "These'll keep you warm."

April felt the material and smiled. "Much warmer!" she exclaimed. "There aren't enough suns here."

May's dress proved similar, but with a red and blue plaid. June's was navy with light blue vertical pinstripes and red piping. They fell upon the new clothes and, without any evidence of shyness, began to change. Fortunately, no one else entered the hallway.

Master D and Raahi turned their backs, looking uncomfortable with the operation. When they finally turned around again, Master D nodded and said, "Very good! Other than those hairdos, you look like proper young ladies from this world now."

"Oh!" Raahi exclaimed. "I wondered who the fourth box was for." Sie had changed too. Her school uniform, which had gotten stained with dirt in the fight with the bees, was replaced by a turquoise dress. She'd gotten a pair of leather boots for herself, too, and a new pair of pale blue stockings. "Let's go," she said. She waved a hand at the discarded clothes and they shimmered out of sight.

"Occluded?" Master D asked.

"Delivered. I sent them to the laundry basket at my Aunt Gen's house. We don't want anyone tripping over invisible clothes or they might get to wondering."

"Very good," Master D said. "However, I cannot condone your shop-lifting tendencies, Silent. What would your aunt say?"

"Exigent circumstances. But feel free to reimburse the store after we've finished our rescue mission," she added.

"I suppose we can let it slip just this once," Master D said. "Shall we head for Newbury Street?"

And then Sie led them down the hallway to where a wide set of stairs came out at a spacious lobby full of comfortable armchairs and large potted plants. She led them across the lobby and out the door then turned and headed for Boston Common.

Their path took them through the Common and over the pedestrian bridge above the pond where the swan boats ply their pleasant trade. Along the way, Sie made the mistake of suggesting that April and her sisters let their hair down.

"We never do that in public!" April exclaimed, and all three of them looked horrified.

"It's just that your hairstyle is, uh, unusual," Sie said. "People are looking at you."

"In admiration!" April said. "Soon everyone in your world will be wearing their hair up, just like us." She reached a hand up to touch the stacked coils. "We do look wonderful, don't we?"

"If you say so," Sie muttered.

TWENTY-SIX

Hidden

The thugs from BAAM marched Ali to a back door of the church and pushed her inside. They hurried her through the dark and dusty interior past construction scaffolding and a pile of wood planks to a platform on which two women were bound hand and foot, sitting back to back on wooden chairs. One was unfamiliar to Ali. The other was Silent's great aunt.

They brought another wooden chair and began to tape her to it.

"Are you all right?" Ali asked, and Aunt Gen nodded. She could not speak. They'd put tape over her mouth.

Before Ali could think of anything else to ask that would be easy to respond to with a nod or shake of the head, one of the boys taped her mouth too.

Then the BAAM students left.

She began to struggle against the tape but could not get out of it.

The boys came back with several more students. With them was a man who had a white beard and mustache and a pointed face with a vulture's beak of a nose. He frowned. "How did she find us?" he demanded.

One of the boys handed him the instrument she'd used.

"Resourceful. Next time we take someone, remember to burn their house. No clues!" He smashed the instrument on the floor and stepped on it. "Right?"

"Yes, master," a chorus of boys said. But the smallest boy actually said, "Yes, Master Saint-Omer."

The man spun around. "Who said that?" he demanded.

The other boys pointed at the youngest one, who looked stricken. "I, I didn't think, sir! I'm sorry! I'll, uh—"

"You're a worthless dog!" the man growled. And the boy was. He fell forward and shrank and shifted shape until he was a wirehaired terrier, brown and white in color, that barked, bent around to stare at itself, then whimpered and ran away.

Saint-Omer sighed. "I'm tired of having to work with these idiotic boys, but it can't be helped."

The other boys were staring, open mouthed. As for Ali, if her mouth hadn't been taped shut, it would have been hanging wide open too.

The woman Ali didn't know renewed her struggle against the tape, but Aunt Gen sat stiffly, her eyes angry, glaring at Master Saint-Omer.

Saint-Omer turned to his captives. "*You* were going to die anyway," he said, addressing Aunt Gen, "since you probably remember me. I certainly remember you! What a lot of trouble you caused me. But that is all in the past, and now it's my turn." He grinned. "Actually," he continued, "now that dog-boy told the rest of the hostages my name, you all have to die. But, I need you alive for a little longer. You're my bait." His eyes settled on Ali. "Too bad this location appears to be compromised. Hmm." He paced back and forth, stroking his beard. "Of course!" he exclaimed. "I'll put you out of temporal sequence! Nothing like hiding you in plain sight." He chuckled.

And then he pulled something out of a pocket.

It looked to Ali like a silver pocket watch. Well, maybe not silver; it was a bit too metallic. Platinum? He snapped the lid open and touched the face. The watch must have had accessible hands because the man seemed to be turning them.

The world began to spin. Ali tried to scream but the tape muffled her. Everything blurred and her stomach cramped painfully. She was spinning in a foggy, airless void.

Her skin crawled with itches that chased sharper prickling pains up and down her limbs. *This must be what it feels like to die,* she thought.

Then, just when it seemed impossible to survive another moment, the spinning slowed and the chair stopped moving. Her feet were on the platform again. She was very dizzy and painfully short of breath. She could hear Miss Lee and the other woman gasping for breath, too, but could not see them. The boys had positioned her with her back to them.

The horrible master and the boys from BAAM were nowhere to be seen.

Very little was to be seen, actually. For some reason, it was as dark as midnight, not only within the church but outside the stained glass windows too.

TWENTY-SEVEN

Raahi Breaks the Code

They made good time in spite of April, May, and June, who found the midday picnickers on Boston Common fascinating and could not stop gawking at every old person they passed. April said she didn't know people could *get* so old. The carriages and cars surprised them too.

"Your flowers are so tiny!" April exclaimed as they walked past a garden bed. "And the bees are miniature too," June added (or was it May?).

Telling them there would be time to explore *after* the hostages were freed, Sie hurried on. Finally they were standing on the busy sidewalk in front of the gallery.

And Raahi was not there.

Raahi was about a block behind them, standing thoughtfully in the middle of the sidewalk. Pedestrians had to go around him, but he didn't seem to notice.

Raahi was thinking about how the bee girls had praised—and kissed— him. Girls didn't usually pay him quite so much attention. In fact, hardly any attention at all. And girls from *his* world—make that *worlds*—didn't talk like that. So singsong and formal. So rehearsed and, well, downright odd! It certainly gave him a lot to think about . . .

"Raahi!" Sie called. "Are you coming?"

By the time he caught up, Sie had already scanned the sidewalk in front of the gallery and reached an unsettling conclusion. There was nothing written in chalk there. Nothing at all. "Do you think we beat them here?" Sie asked as Raahi hurried to join them.

Master D frowned. "Perhaps they're still waiting at the library in hope of intercepting us."

"Or maybe they're hiding nearby and watching," Raahi said, "to check out our bee-world visitor. April, can you, uh, do that thing with your sisters now?"

"If you think it's important, boy," she said.

"It is."

"We need room to spin," April added. "Could you block the path?"

"The sidewalk?" Sie asked. "Sure."

Silent and Master D directed pedestrians around them, saying, "Excuse us, please, these girls wish to dance." At least that's what Master D said. Sie just glared at people and put her hands on her hips. Startled, they stepped around her and hurried on while April, May, and June spun into a blur of new dresses and shiny boots going round and round. And then there was just one.

Sie raised an eyebrow. April was now wearing a dress that seemed to be made of quilted patches from all three dresses. Together they made for a rather difficult-to-look-at pattern.

"We're all here," April announced, smoothing the unusual dress.

"I can see that," Sie said. "Raahi, do you sense anyone?"

"Spying on us, you mean?" he asked.

"Exactly," Sie said.

"Actually, I *do* feel someone's eyes on us. Do you see anyone suspicious?"

"I don't," Master D said, "however, my watch is reading in the danger zone again." He gave it a shake, studied it, then frowned and replaced it in his pocket.

"Can I talk to you in private, Sie?" Raahi asked. He had come up beside Sie and spoken in a whisper.

"Now?"

"Shh. Yes. Let's tell them we're going across the street to take a look around. Uh, wait here, please," he said in a louder voice. "We're going to search the other side of the street."

"You could've just said that first," Sie remarked as they darted in front of a slow-moving carriage and hurried to the opposite sidewalk.

"*Now* do you see anyone?" Raahi asked. "I still feel like I'm being watched."

"No. What do you want to talk about?"

"Do you know how to block the bee girls' magic?" he asked.

"Like how we warded against the stasis spell?" Sie replied.

"No, I mean, can you stop them from doing any magic at all?"

"I'm not sure. Maybe if they were sick and too weak, but that's not very nice," Sie pointed out. "Why?"

"Because this is another trap."

Sie stared at him. "What kind of a trap?"

"I'm not exactly sure, but the queen bee *wants* us to send the girls to the Hunt Club."

"She does? How do you know that?" Sie demanded, glancing across the street at April, who was happily twirling in her new three-patterns-in-one dress.

"And," Raahi continued, lowering his voice, "I'm pretty sure they're still linked to her somehow. That patch of bee fur on their necks was a diversion put there to draw our attention away from whatever the real link is."

"You're scaring me," Sie said. "But you don't have evidence for any of this, do you?"

"Of course I do. Weren't you listening?"

"To what?"

"To *them*, when they were, uh, you know . . ."

"Pawing you?"

"It was just so they could deliver a coded message. Well, even if they *do* like me, it was mostly for show. By the way, do you think your friend Ali, uh, well, do you think she might have a little bit of a crush on me?"

"*What* message?" Sie demanded, an eyebrow arching expressively.

"Oh. Right. Remember how they wanted to thank me, all *three* of them? They kept repeating variations on the number three. And do you remember what they said?"

"I was distracted by how all over you they were, actually." She gave him a withering look.

"Yes, but listen to the message when I emphasize every third word: 'We can't **wait** to help **you**. And we **can't** believe you **trust** all of **us**. Without those **patches** that we **were** wearing, we're **not** slaves, for **real**.' See?"

"So the real message was 'Wait, you can't trust us. Patches were not real.'" Sie stared at him. "That's not good."

"And then June said, 'We three **just** wanted to **be** clear and **careful** to say, **because** you're not **enemies**, and we **are** to go **everywhere** with you.'"

"Just be careful because enemies are everywhere," Sie translated. "What do you think it all means?"

"I think," Raahi said, "that the Hunt Club is cooperating with the queen bee. A gang of kids is just what she'd need to take over this world using bee magic. Saint-Omer might not realize that he's a means to that end— just like we are. We brought her bee-soldiers right to the Hunt Club!"

Sie frowned. "And?"

"And the queen's choice of April was clever, since we fell for the sentimental appeal of bringing her sisters along with her, which means that we just inserted three deadly otherworlders into downtown Boston."

"With three of them, they may well be strong enough to take over," Sie said. "Especially with the help of the Hunt Club. The faculty of Linacre College didn't do so well against April." Sie bit her lip. "*This* is a *big* problem," she concluded. "*Another* big problem."

"No kidding," Raahi replied. "Ideas?"

"One thing's for sure," Sie said. "We can't let April reach the Hunt Club. But without her, how are we going to do the trade?"

"You're good at illusions," Raahi pointed out.

"Illusions only do what you instruct them to in advance. We don't know how they'll test April before they let the hostages go. It has to be a real live person."

"Then can you make one person look like another?" Raahi asked. "I could pretend to be—"

"Yes, but you're not going in there," Sie said, sounding quite firm. "They'll just beat you up again or worse. I could go."

"No need," Raahi said, smiling as he squinted across the street to where April and Master D were waiting. "We have a real live Custodian with us. Let's send Master D."

"What if he doesn't agree, and how are we going to explain it to him without April hearing?" Sie asked.

"We aren't. I've got a new plan."

"You'd better have a good one," Sie said. "And you'll have to whisper it in my ear because someone's spying on us from those bushes over there."

TWENTY-EIGHT

Chauncey

There was an iron fence in front of the house opposite the gallery, close to where Sie and Raahi were standing. Behind the iron fence was a garden of tall bushes. And those bushes were rustling.

"Someone's trying to get closer to us," Sie whispered. "To hear what we're saying."

Raahi nodded. "So," he said, rather loudly. "What are we going to do if no one shows up to tell us where to go next?"

"I don't know," Sie said, also in a loud voice. "I'm just going to look around. Maybe they meant *this* side of the street, not the other." She was working her way toward the suspicious rustling as she spoke. With a quick motion, her arm disappeared into the bushes, then she pulled it back. Her hand was grasping the shirt of a boy about her height with horn-rimmed glasses and curly brown hair.

"Ow!" he exclaimed. She'd tugged him up against the fence.

"It's Chauncey," Raahi said. "He watched while the others beat me up. How are you doing, Chauncey? Missing your big friends now?"

"I'm trained in dueling and I'm not afraid to—ow! Don't pull so hard!"

"You're in Master Saint-Omer's dueling class, aren't you?" Raahi asked.

"That's right! So tell her to let go of me before I—"

"Which has met, what, two times?" Raahi said. "How many duels have you fought? *She's* fought *lots* of duels. Maybe you should do what she says."

Chauncey did not have a reply to that.

"Okay," Raahi said. "Here's what you're going to do. You're going to tell us exactly where they're holding my mother and Sie's aunt."

"Let go of me!" Chauncey cried, struggling against Sie's grip again.

"Sure thing," she said and let him go. But before he could duck back behind the bushes, she wove a micro-whirlwind that beat madly against the foliage as it lifted him over the fence and deposited him on the sidewalk. "I can send you fifty feet up," she said. She leaned close to his frightened face. "And drop you!"

"If you say so," he whimpered. "But Master Saint-Omer's going to take care of both of you!"

"We'll see about that. Where are they, and why didn't anyone leave us instructions?" Sie demanded.

Chauncey produced a piece of chalk from his pocket. "I'm supposed to write them down, but not yet. They said to wait an hour and then send you to . . . Actually, I can't tell you for another forty-five minutes. Sorry, but I don't dare go against the master. He'll—ow! My feet!"

Sie smiled. "Yes, they've sunk into the sidewalk, and yes, they are being squeezed painfully. A little payback for when your master's brother did that to us. But so far it's just to hold you in place. If I get upset, they'll be squeezed so hard you'll never walk again. Do you plan to upset me?" She glared at him.

"People might notice," Raahi said, sounding nervous.

"Not a problem. I've put a concealment and a diversion around us. Listen very carefully, Chauncey. If I don't like your answers, I'll increase the pressure. And if you send us to the wrong place . . ." She demonstrated by pressing her hands together. "Splat! Now, where are you supposed to send us in forty-five minutes?"

"Ow! Okay, okay! The message is 'Take the alien to the church.'"

"*The* church?" Sie's eyes narrowed dangerously. "Do you know how many churches there are in Back Bay? I can't even count."

"I, I was supposed to remember the name of it, but you frightened me so now I can't." He winced, no doubt expecting the pressure to increase.

Sie paused, then, her expression softening, reached out to cup his face in her hand. "You poor thing," she crooned. "The youngest in the gang. I'm sure they aren't very nice to you. And now I'm treating you badly too." Here, she let off most of the pressure on his feet. "Is that more comfortable? I'm sorry, but this will all be over soon." She smiled.

"Uh, th-thanks. Much better, actually."

"I'm sure it'll be all right if we just let you go after we find out which church," she continued. Her hand went to his shoulder and rested gently there. "Do you remember *anything* about the church?"

"Uh, uh, I think it's Episcopal," he said.

"Episcopal. Very good!" She gave his shoulder a little pat. "And where is it?"

"They said you'd know it."

"I'd know it . . . Raahi!" she exclaimed, stepping back. "I bet it's the one Auntie and I go to. It's just down the street—but it's under construction this year."

"That would make it perfect for hiding hostages," Raahi said.

"True." Sie eyed the younger boy. "Good work, Chauncey. The first good work you've ever done, I'll bet. Wait here."

"Ow! My feet! It's tighter now! You said you'd let me go!"

"I lied. What's the expression? Fight fire with fire. But I suppose you might attract attention once I let the concealment slip. Hmm. Let's see . . . This could be tricky, but . . . ." She glanced across the street to where Master D and the patchwork April were standing then raised both arms and, her eyes fluttering closed, muttered a lengthy incantation. There was a pause in things. Passing pedestrians seemed not to be moving, the leaves on the trees stopped rustling and the horse-drawn carriages and antique motorcars on the road slowed to a stop and went quiet. Then there was a flash of bright light, leaving Raahi blinking, before everything went back to normal.

Except Chauncey. He was gone. There were two shoe-shaped dents in the sidewalk where his feet had sunk in, but no Chauncey.

The only other change Raahi could see was that a dog had appeared. It was about knee high and covered in curly brown hair. It was chewing on a pair of horn-rimmed glasses like the ones Chauncey had been wearing.

"Okay, let's go get Master D and April and head to the church," Sie said, sounding matter of fact.

"Did you actually turn him into a *dog*?" Raahi demanded as they crossed the street. The dog followed.

"Yes. Next question?"

"Do you plan to turn him back?"

"We'll see how things work out."

"You could get in trouble for doing magic like that."

"We're *already* in *lots* of trouble, in case you hadn't noticed. And I had to guarantee he wouldn't talk."

"All he'll be able to do is bark," Raahi said.

"Exactly," Sie said. She was approaching Master D and April, who were waiting in front of the gallery. "I made the switch at the same time," she added, addressing only Raahi.

"Find any clues over there?" April asked as they approached. "Wait, why is my voice so high?"

"You're temporarily a girl, Master D," Sie said. "A bee girl. Get used to it."

"What did you do to us!" April demanded from Master D's body. "I'm an *over* now—and my sisters are stuck in this body with me!"

"You're a respectable gentleman, so don't carry on about it," Sie said. "And no, you can't change yourself back."

"I can and I will," she complained. "I don't like this at all! I'm going to . . ." Her voice trailed off and a puzzled expression came onto her (now Master D's) face.

"You won't be able to talk from now on," Sie said.

The false Master D that was April and her sisters scowled and tried to pull their hands out of their pockets, but they seemed to be stuck.

"Locked into the pockets," Sie explained. "No waving hands to form runes. We need you for appearances' sake, but you won't be doing *anything*. Is that clear?"

April nodded Master D's head reluctantly.

"Uh, I confess I'm impressed by the power of your illusions, Silent," Master D said in April's high voice, "but would you mind explaining what your intentions are, because this is highly irregular if I do say—"

"Don't say," Sie interrupted. "You're talking like a professor when you're disguised as a girl. And they aren't illusions. You're temporarily in a transformed body. Best to be thorough when dealing with someone as experienced as Saint-Omer. All right, this way, everyone. And Raahi, stop patting that dog!"

Sie headed off at a fast pace and Raahi followed, tugging the new April after him. But the fake Master D who was actually the bee girls came along more slowly, looking very unhappy.

TWENTY-NINE

A Hole
in Emmanuel Church

Raahi assumed Sie was heading for the tall steeple up ahead, but she aimed for a smaller and older church in its shadow. They could see, across a hedge and narrow lawn, a set of double doors in an arched entry. There was a sign that said "Closed for Construction."

"This is it," she said, eyeing the quiet exterior. "They must be holding them in there."

"So you've brought us our alien, after all!" It was not one of the boys this time; it was Saint-Omer himself. He had shimmered into view on the lawn in front of the church. "And ahead of schedule! Did you really think I wouldn't be keeping watch?"

Sie turned and whispered something to Master D, who had just caught up. They (April, May, and June in Master D's body) pouted and shook their head, but Sie whispered again and they shrugged. "Only because you insist," they muttered as they stepped forward. After another annoyed glance at Sie, they said what she had told them to say, although without enthusiasm: "As a Senior Custodian, I order you to release the hostages at once."

Master Saint-Omer burst into laughter. "Really?" he finally managed to say. "That's all you've got, Dorsenhaal? Haven't recovered from our last encounter, have you? But at least you followed my instructions and brought me my alien." He turned to face April. "Come!" There was a roar as flame erupted in a circle behind him. They could see, through its center, the dark interior of the church. He pointed at April (or the person he *thought* was her) and, with a *whoosh*, she was sucked toward him and they both disappeared through the flaming hole. Then the flame winked out and the hole was gone, leaving nothing but a cloud of sooty smoke that wafted away across the front lawn.

As soon as Saint-Omer and his latest captive disappeared, a tremendous clap of thunder rent the air above the church, followed by loud rumblings—and by at least a hundred darting bolts of lightning. They struck everywhere in the little lawn and garden in front of the church, digging burnt furrows in the grass and destroying the shrubbery.

They also struck the three figures who were standing there. Repeatedly. The bodies of Silent, Raahi, and the fake Master D danced and smoked horribly as the lightning tossed and spun them before throwing them cruelly to the ground, where they lay, charred and smoking, on the burnt lawn. (The dog had run away.)

"It's just what you suspected," Raahi said, frowning. "He was planning to kill us as soon as he got April." They were hiding behind a parked carriage out on Newbury Street. They'd sent illusions to deliver the fake bee girl.

"I'm going to have to leave our corpses there for a little while, in case he sends someone to check that we're dead," Sie said.

The bee girls, inside the form of Master D, said nothing because Sie's block was still on them, but they were shaking and staring wide-eyed.

"That's your ally," Sie said, studying them. "Next time you might give a little more thought to who you work with."

"Shh," Raahi warned. "I hear the door latch unlocking. Someone's coming out."

They ducked down again as Rudy leaned out the front door and took in the carnage. He smiled happily and withdrew, latching the door behind him.

"He'll report our deaths," Sie said, waving a hand. The illusionary bodies shimmered and disappeared. "So far so good. Now we have to sneak in and get the hostages out without anyone noticing. April, you and your sisters will wait here while Raahi and I—"

"Not so fast." It was, to their surprise, April's voice. They spun around. The fake Master D was no longer there. Somehow April had escaped Sie's form-shift and so had her sisters, who were flanking her, hands raised, ready to form runes.

"Just great!" Raahi exclaimed. "Can this day get any worse?"

"Blocks!" Sie called as the girls took aim.

Raahi, once again, was too slow. He stood there, an alarmed expression frozen on his face, immobilized by a stasis rune.

"Sorry, girl," April said, and she sounded like she actually *was* sorry, "but we have our directs, you see, and we can't disobey or we'll be punished through the link." They raised their hands in unison and began marking another rune in the air.

Sie didn't recognize the rune, which meant she didn't know how to block it, so she threw herself to the sidewalk and rolled, wondering how there could still be a link to the queen.

Icicles clattered down around her, some of them poking her painfully. It was an ice spell and it would have frozen her solid if it had hit her straight on.

She rolled out into the street just as a team of horses came trotting past with a large carriage behind them. Her roll took her between the front and rear wheels of the carriage and onto the other side of Newbury Street, when she jumped up, bruised and out of breath, to face her three identical enemies.

That was when the dog that had been Chauncey rushed up and bit her leg, growling and holding on tight.

To master the art of dueling, suspend yourself from the mundane details of attack and defense and seek the higher viewpoint. Sie recalled the statement precisely. It had been the one and only thing a visiting so-called Zen expert had said when she gave a talk on dueling at GALA last semester. She'd stood at the podium in silence for several long minutes before speaking that one sentence, bowing, and walking out of the hall and all the way out of the school, never to be seen again. The students had been stunned at first, and then the assembly hall had filled with nervous laughter until the headmistress hurried to the podium and dismissed them with an apology for "our eccentric but very eminent visitor." Sie had not understood at all what the expert had meant. But for some reason, through the searing pain of the dog bite and with the awareness that April, May, and June were about to deliver another attack, those words came back to her.

I don't think she meant 'higher viewpoint' literally, Sie thought. *But why not?* And then she levitated herself a hundred feet in the air.

The dog held on for just a moment, but it was enough to be pulled six feet up (with Sie clenching her teeth in pain), so that when it fell, it hit the ground hard, yelped, and went running down the street, tail between its legs.

Dripping blood from her ankle, Sie rose high into the air as the bee girls' runes shot under her and struck a horse that was pulling an open carriage. The horse stopped abruptly, swayed, and fell over in the road with a tremendous thump. The driver jumped clear with a shout of surprise and ran off in the same direction as the dog.

Sie began to fall because, of course, what goes up must come down. *But not too fast*, she thought, hurrying to weave a supporting wind that would hold her in place about fifty feet above the sidewalk. She could see the triplets' heads down below her, their odd beehive hairstyles pointing up.

Then they realized what she'd done and tipped their pointed spirals of hair back as they raised their eyes to study her.

"If I put you in stasis up there," April called, "you'll fall to the ground and break every bone in your body, so why don't you just come down here and surrender?"

"I doubt the queen bee wants to take me captive. More likely she wants me dead," Sie said from high above. "Your hair," she added, frowning. "It's very odd, actually, isn't it?"

April paused before replying, and when she spoke, it was in the same sing-song manner that she'd used when she'd given Raahi his coded warning: "Leave our *hair* alone! It *is* our special *secret* hairstyle, so *please* do not *loosen* our favorite *hairbands*, girl!"

"Everyone else I saw in your world had their hair down," Sie said, thinking out loud. "You're actually the only ones wearing beehive hairdos."

"Mistress says we have to eliminate you right now," April announced. "Sorry about that." And then they began to form more runes.

Sie wove another wind. It burst down the sidewalk, flapped the girls' dresses madly and, as Sie concentrated to focus and strengthen it, tugged their hair out. With a grunt of effort, Sie pushed harder and the wind whistled angrily, freeing the wiry ties from their hair. Their hair, it turned out, was quite long, and the wind was having fun playing with it.

Sie let herself down beside the immobile Raahi. "So," she said, studying April closely, "was I right?"

May and June stared at Silent in disbelief, and April, tears springing to her eyes, rushed forward and threw her arms around her. It wasn't an attack. It was a grateful hug. "I can't believe you figured it out!" she exclaimed. "You saved us! May, June, come here and show Sie how grateful we are!"

"No, please, no!" Sie exclaimed, pushing them away. "Those ties, they were pieces of bee antenna, weren't they?"

"Yes!" April exclaimed, trying to give her another hug, but Sie held out an arm to stop her. "That's how Mistress really keeps control of us. Everyone gets a length of bee antenna and our very first direction is to never take it off. I usually wear mine as a bracelet, but Mistress thought you'd notice so she made us put them in our hair. No one messes with your hair if you do it neatly enough, right?"

"Of course. And those fuzzy patches?"

"That hurt! Mistress used magic to make the hairs sink in so you'd think that's how she directed us. She took it from a worker bee. Clever, isn't she?"

"And now you're *really* free of her?" Sie asked.

"Yes!" April exclaimed. She turned and took the stasis off Raahi, who stumbled forward, did a double take at the sight of the triplets with their hair down, then rushed to form a warding rune in the air.

"A little late, boy," April said, looking amused. "But we still like you."

"You betrayed us!" Raahi exclaimed. "Although, come to think of it, you *did* give us a coded warning. Was that so the queen wouldn't realize?"

"I did what I could, but it had to be clever and secret," April said. "Sorry, boy. Want us to kiss you again? May, June, shall we?"

"No! I believe you. Uh, now what?" he added, turning to Sie.

"We have to find the hostages before the Hunt Club realizes we gave them a fake April," Sie said.

"You won't be much good with an injury like that," April pointed out. She leaned down and formed complex shapes in the air in front of Sie's bleeding dog bite. "Is that better?" she asked. "I studied magical first aid in my explorer training."

"Much better, thanks," Sie said.

"I *hope* this means they're finally free of the queen," Raahi said, frowning. "But she's proven to be a clever enemy, and under her direction the bee girls' behavior has been consistently deceptive to date."

"Did the boy just invite us on a date?" April asked.

"Uh, um, not exactly," Raahi stuttered, starting to flush.

"Do you do air-weavings?" Sie asked April.

"We can do liftings, if that's what you mean," April said.

"Sounds like the same thing," Sie said. "I'll lift Raahi. You three follow."

"Lift me where?" Raahi exclaimed, sounding alarmed.

"Okay, this is a *very* simple plan," Sie continued. "I'd feel bad about it except that, hey, they already have a contractor working here, so what's one more hole? And if our goal is to surprise our enemies, then a rapid entry is best."

"Now, wait just one minute," Raahi objected. "That's *very* risky! Lots of things can go wr—*Hey!*" Without waiting for him to finish,

Sie had summoned a cushion of air and lifted both of them. April and her sisters, forming runes with their hands, teetered up and whooshed along after.

They floated over the gate and aimed for the bushes growing against the church's front wall. Raahi winced in anticipation of the impact, but just before they reached the wall, Sie wove a final burst of air and a hole appeared with a tremendous *ka-bang.* They swooshed into the church and landed in the central aisle with dusty pews on either side.

In front of them, up near the altar, Master Saint-Omer and a group of boys were circled around Master D.

"Sorry!" Master D exclaimed when he saw them. "They realized I was a fake and changed me back."

"Well, well!" Master Saint-Omer exclaimed. "I see you faked your own deaths. A clever deception, I'll give you that much, but it won't help you. Aliens, kill the unwanted ones!"

April, May, and June exchanged glances. "As you wish," April said. "But it's too bad for you that we're free from our directs so *we* can decide who's not wanted." She began to form a rune with her hands.

As April, May, and June hurled their workings at Master Saint-Omer and the Hunt Club, Master D ducked down and hurried toward Silent and Raahi. "They were torturing me!" he complained.

"Thanks for going in," Raahi said. "Are you all right?"

"I'll probably live," he grumbled. "But don't tell anyone that you turned me into a girl!"

"What's wrong with girls?" Sie demanded. "And why aren't you helping the bee girls in the fight?" She gave him a push in their direction.

"It looks like April, May, and June have them pinned down," Raahi said. "Let's go find Maa and Aunt Gen."

"Do you know," Sie said, "Sir John Ninian Comper? He's a British architect."

"Are you making fun of me?" Raahi demanded. "Because it's hardly the t—"

"He designs churches in high Gothic style," Sie continued. "And he's been retained to design the new chapel they're building here. Auntie helped raise the money to bring him to Boston."

"You *do* remember that we need to find the hostages?" Raahi asked.

"Auntie is very interested in the stained glass windows. One of them, the oldest one, is rather odd," Sie continued.

"In what way?" Master D asked. He was following them, despite Sie's instructions.

"Don't forget the hostages," Raahi interjected. "We can discuss antique windows later."

"This window has a shield in its center with Saint George's Cross, and on either side of that, the Greek symbols for alpha and omega," Sie said.

"Heavens!" Master D looked startled. "Why would they have a window that evokes the worst abuses of the Crusades? The red cross of St. George was carried into battle, of course, and the alpha for beginning and omega for end represent the idea of conquering all worlds from nearest to farthest."

"It seems," Sie said, "that troublemakers of one sort or another have been plotting to take over the world for a long time. And I bet Saint-Omer was attracted to that window. Isn't his name associated with the Knights Templar? He's probably a descendant of the original crusaders."

"Well, now," Master D said. "I suppose there are certain occasions where erudition is entirely appropriate. I'm reminded of several historical anecdotes myself, such as—"

"This way, Raahi," Sie interrupted. "And Master D, stop talking and *go help the bee girls!*" Then she ducked under some scaffolding and led Raahi through the dim light, turning a corner and entering the oldest section of the church.

THIRTY

Dead Ends

As soon as they came into view of the window with its bright red cross high on the wall, they saw Aunt Gen and Raahi's mother sitting back to back, taped to wooden chairs. And, inexplicably, there was Ali, taped tightly to a chair as well.

Raahi and Sie began to run toward them, but Master D called, "Wait!" He had followed them again, instead of joining the bee girls in the fight.

"Why?" Sie demanded.

"Too simple," he said. "And if it seems too good to be true . . ."

"It probably *is* too good to be true," Raahi finished, frowning. "Maa, are you all right?"

She did not reply.

"Aunt Gen?" Sie called. "Ali?" But they did not reply either. In fact, they weren't even moving.

"Stasis spell?" Raahi asked.

"They wouldn't know how yet," Sie said. "They haven't gotten hold of bee magic. Let's have a closer look."

"Wait." Master D had his pocket watch out again. He tapped it, held it to his ear, frowned at it, then clicked it closed. "We're at a major confluence."

"Confluence of what?" Raahi demanded.

"Different probabilities, all converging here. However," he said, taking a few steps toward the immobile hostages, "they are not."

"Not what?" Sie demanded.

"Not here. This is an illusion."

"I'm going to see," Sie said, striding toward the captives.

"Don't step on it!" Master D called as Sie approached the low wooden platform on which the chairs rested.

Sie paused, her foot in the air. "Why not?"

"The danger needle is spinning wildly," Master D said. "That platform probably has a bomb under it or something of the sort."

"A bomb? How unmagical," Sie said, sounding disgusted. "What am I supposed to do about that?"

"Send it somewhere?" Raahi suggested.

"Good idea. I'll just put it under the Hunt Club to help April and her sisters with their fight." The platform disappeared, but the three illusionary hostages still sat on their chairs, floating six inches above the floor.

"Move that bomb out onto the lawn, please," Master D said. "We may need to take Saint-Omer and his boys alive in order to find out where they hid the hostages."

"If I must." Sie closed her eyes and concentrated. There was a shout of surprise from around the corner, and then the sounds of fighting resumed, but they were soon drowned out by a loud *ka-**bang*** from just outside the building. The floor shook and a crack appeared in the old stained glass window.

And then the sounds of fighting faded, a door slammed in the distance, and it grew quiet in the old church.

The bee girls came in sight. "We chased them away," April said. "But my sisters got sprayed."

"Sprayed?" Sie frowned. "Are they hurt?"

"Worse," April said. "They can't do magic."

Master D hurried to examine them. "Platinum-world tech," he said. "Don't touch them. The compound is still on their clothes. It blocks your magic. We ran into it years ago in Egypt."

"Will it wear off?" Raahi asked.

Master D shrugged. "Depends on the dose. May and June are going to be sidelined for now at least. April, you'd better stay here at the church with them. They're defenseless on their own. We'll come back once we've freed the hostages, assuming we can find them, of course."

"Did you see which way the Hunt Club went?" Sie asked.

April shrugged. "They got in a carriage and raced away. There was a powerful ward around it. I couldn't stop it."

"If only we had a tracker," Master D said. "But they are very rare."

"What about the one at GALA?" Sie asked.

Master D shook his head. "It's on loan from the Boston Custodian because it got damaged and doesn't track properly anymore. I don't think there's another to be had here in Boston, unless your aunt still has hers?"

"You're standing on it," Sie said. "It's broken." She'd leaned over to pick up something. "Ali must've used it with this writing quill." She handed the broken quill to Master D, who slipped it into his jacket pocket. "She probably went to look for me and realized that Auntie had been kidnapped." Sie paused to study the three illusions. "Now she's in danger too."

"We'll find them," Raahi said.

"How?" Sie asked.

"Sisters?" April asked. "I think it's time."

"Time for what?" Master D asked.

"Our 'Bee Peppy!' chant. We do it whenever we're in hopeless situations," April said with a grin.

"Hopeless?" Sie repeated. "Do you really think so?"

"No!" April exclaimed. "That's what the chant's for. Come on, girls! One, two, one-two-three! Oh, **bee** happy, **bee** peppy, **bee** certain, **bee** sweet! **We** know, **we're** confident, **we** can't **bee** beat! **Hurray**!" They had performed this along with animated movements, and now they stood grinning widely, their arms extended upward and their hands in triumphant fists.

"A *cheer*?" Sie stared at them. "At a time like *this*?"

"It gets us motivated," April said. "Okay, sisters, pick up the pieces!" And then they got down on their hands and knees and began to collect tiny brass and glass shards.

THIRTY-ONE

Bee-ing Brilliant

Master D pulled one of the floating chairs out of the illusion. At first his hand went right through it, but then he muttered something and, on the next try, it actually *was* a chair. He set it down next to where Raahi and Silent were standing. "That's better," he said.

"*What's* better?" Sie demanded. "It seems to me that everything is actually much worse."

"I meant the chair, but I do think we have reason to hope."

"Pardon me for interrupting," Raahi said, "but we still don't know where the hostages are and they have a third hostage now. What's better about that?"

"Nothing," Sie said.

Master D nodded. "But on the positive side, now we understand their plot. And thanks to you, Sie, the bee girls are on our side." He glanced over to where April, May, and June were on their hands and knees, picking up bits of broken tracker. "Also, we learned that we are at least an even match to our enemies."

"How so?" Raahi asked.

"We're still alive and they had to run away, which gives me confidence that we may win next time."

"Did *you* do anything in the fight?" Sie asked.

"Oh, well, I cast a few blocks and wards. The air was thick with workings. Very dangerous, I must say!"

Raahi and Sie exchanged a look.

"Excuse me, sir," Raahi said, "but do you actually fight? Or is your magic more of a defensive nature?"

"Well . . ."

"You don't!" Sie exclaimed. "Which means you left it to April, May, and June! No wonder two of them were badly injured!"

"They're fine," Master D said. "Not a scratch."

"They can't do magic," Sie hissed, glaring at him. "So obviously, they're *not* fine! And *you* don't seem to be much use in a fight. What's that about?"

"Well, I'm retired."

"And why is that?" Sie demanded.

"It's a bit complicated," Master D said. "Otherworld magic and so forth. You know how it is."

"Why don't you tell us how it is?" Raahi asked before Sie could explode. She looked like she wanted to strangle someone.

Master D sighed. "It goes back to Egypt. All of this does. You see, Master Saint-Omer was actually a student in the original Hunt Club, along with his brother and a half dozen others. They were stopped when they were at BAAM, but a decade later they discovered a doorway into a world in which platinum-based magic was practiced. Quite a few instruments and weapons were smuggled into Egypt, I'm afraid."

"Like the spray they used on May and June?" Raahi asked.

"Yes. And I was telling only a partial truth when I said the effect wears off. It may not wear off entirely."

"Were you sprayed?" Sie asked.

He nodded. "And more. They forced me to swallow some of the compound. Held my mouth open and sprayed it down my throat. I've never been quite the same. That's why I left active duty on a CRACK team and took up the teaching position."

"That's too bad," Sie said with a frown.

"I appreciate your sympathy."

"I didn't mean it that way," she said. "You should've been honest with us. Not knowing our true strength, or *weakness*, was a handicap. Now we're down to three out of six!"

"So what are we going to—" Raahi began to say.

April interrupted. "There!" she exclaimed. "All the pieces. We even got some from in between the floorboards." Her hands were full of tiny broken bits of the instrument.

Raahi raised an eyebrow, Master D frowned, and Sie sighed.

"What?" April seemed surprised by their lack of enthusiasm.

"It has to be intact to work," Sie said.

"Right!" April smiled and began to spin. She spun and spun, like when she'd folded her sisters into herself, but this time they stood back and, to Sie and Raahi's horror, cheered her on. "Bee brilliant, bee bright, bee clever, don't bite!" they chanted as they danced excitedly, waving their arms above their heads.

"Oh my God," Sie said.

"Bees don't bite; they sting," Raahi pointed out.

"That's correct," April said, coming out of her spin to stop in front of him. She was smiling. "The chant's about doing things right and *making* things right. Thanks, sisters! Oh, and here you go." She handed something to Raahi.

He was so surprised that he nearly dropped it.

"Hey!" Sie reached over and grabbed it. "Auntie's tracker! How did you do that?"

"You can say thanks now," April said.

"Thanks. Uh, that was brilliant, actually," Sie conceded. "Now we just need something to track them *with*." She opened the little drawer.

"This must've worked the first time," Master D said. He was holding the broken quill they'd found on the floor. "Your aunt's, I presume."

"Yes." Sie closed it in the drawer. "The needle's turning," she said. "It's still turning. It's spinning around and, uh, not stopping."

"Let me see," Master D said, getting to his feet. "Oh dear. It may be damaged."

Sie set it down on the chair. If she hadn't had a stern personal rule about it, she probably would have teared up a little.

"Sorry," April said.

"Not your fault," Sie said. "Good try."

"It's *still* spinning," Master D said with a frown. "I wonder what that means?"

"It means we need to think," Raahi said. He reached out for another of the illusionary chairs but his hand went right through it. "Hey, if your magic's gone, how did you make your chair solid?" he demanded.

"I used a transformation," Master D said. "It's a working that pulls mass from the surrounding area, but I'm not sure of the exact physics."

"No, I mean, how did *you* do it," Raahi said, "since your magic's blocked?"

"Oh. Well, it's funny but when I forget myself and do something semiautomatically, then my magic actually works. Wards tend to be that way, fortunately. After so many duels in the line of duty, I automatically block when someone attacks. But to counter with my own attack requires that I consciously form a strategy and come up with an appropriate working of my own. That's where the platinum spray gives me the most trouble."

"Then we'll leave you in charge of defense," Raahi said. "Just make sure you're standing in front of us in the next fight."

"In front of? Well, I suppose I could. To allow you to focus on your attack, correct?"

"Precisely," Raahi said. "And I'm sorry the tracker's not working," he continued, "but I think it's obvious where we should go next."

"It is?" Master D asked.

"Saint-Omer's study," Raahi said. "Clearly it's their base. If we don't find them there, at least we can look for clues."

"You're going to their hive?" April asked.

Raahi nodded. "But you should stay here with your sisters."

"You should not go to their hive," April said.

"It's not actually a hive," Sie said.

"But it is! They're strongest there, right?" April asked.

"Probably," Raahi said.

"Then unless you trick them somehow, you'll be beaten," April said. "Our queen likes to wait to attack a hive until most of the bees are away. But *your* enemies will be waiting."

They didn't have an answer to that.

THIRTY-TWO

Time

The tape on Ali's mouth was extremely annoying and somewhat painful, but there was enough slack that she could draw some of it in. It tasted disgusting, but after a while she managed to bite a hole in it. Then she struggled to expand the hole by forcing her mouth open, despite the fact that the tape pulled painfully on her skin. "There!" she finally exclaimed. "I can talk!"

"Mmfff." It was Raahi's mother.

"Mmmf!" Aunt Gen added her voice, such as it was.

Clearly being able to talk was not going to do Ali much good without someone to talk to. *Although,* she thought, *if I can do a working to get rid of the rest of the tape . . .* She spoke the words to dissolve the adhesive, but nothing happened. She tried again. Then she tried breaking the chair. That didn't seem to work, either. "I'm sorry," she said. "I can't seem to do magic. They sprayed me with something."

"Mmm hmm," Aunt Gen said.

"Hmmm," Raahi's mother added. And then she began rocking back and forth on her chair.

"Watch out!" Ali exclaimed as Raahi's mother's chair hit hers. "Oh!" she cried when the chairs collided again and she almost tipped over. And then she began rocking back and forth too.

It took some time and they were breathing hard, but finally Raahi's mother and Ali tipped over.

"Ow!" Ali exclaimed. With her hands taped behind her back, she'd been unable to break her fall. Now she was lying on her side with a sore elbow.

"Mmmf!" Raahi's mother said from where she'd fallen beside Ali. And then she began to spin herself slowly around until her back was facing Ali.

"What are you doing?" Ali asked, but of course it wasn't helpful to ask someone whose mouth was taped, so Ali had to wait.

After turning herself around, Raahi's mother began wiggling until her taped hands were in front of Ali's face.

"Oh!" Ali said. "Hang on." And then she wiggled and squirmed until she'd gotten so close that she could get her teeth on the tape. "Yuck!" she said as she spat out a sticky scrap. "It tastes awful!" But she kept going, gnawing and tearing and nibbling, until she'd fought her way through the tape. "Try pulling now," she said.

And it worked! Raahi's mother's hands were free.

It didn't take her long to pull the tape off her feet and crawl away from the tipped-over chair. Then she was on her feet and hurrying to free Aunt Gen.

What about me? Ali thought.

When both women were standing and free of their wrist and ankle bindings, they took a moment to peel the tape off their mouths. It must've hurt because they gasped as it came off. Then they rushed to untape Ali.

"Let me help you with that," Raahi's mother said, taking hold of one end of the tape on Ali's face.

"Ow! I'll do it," Ali said.

"May I?" Aunt Gen asked, placing a hand gently over the tape and muttering something in Latin.

The tape fell away.

"Thanks! Did you dissolve the glue?"

"That's right," Aunt Gen said. "And now I think it's time for introductions. Altheia, this is Mrs. Mishra, Raahi's mother. Monali, this is Ali, Silent's best friend from school."

"Pleased to meet you," Mrs. Mishra said with a smile. "Sorry for the circumstances."

"How did they get you?" Ali asked.

"Three boys came to my door," Mrs. Mishra explained. "They said Raahi had been hurt and I had to come with them. I was worried about him since he hadn't come home after school, so of course I went with them."

"You live in the modern world," Ali pointed out. "How did they get to your house?"

"And how did they get you here?" Aunt Gen added. "We haven't had a chance to talk until now," she explained to Ali.

"I hardly know," Mrs. Mishra said. "They bustled me into the back seat of a car, pinned my arms to my sides, and pulled a cloth bag over my head. I didn't see where we went after that, but at some point they forced me into another car. It seemed antique from the sound of the engine. Then they unloaded me outside this church and marched me in."

"Did you get a look at the car when you got out?"

"Just a glimpse. They pulled the bag off my head as we came in the front door. It *was* an antique. Maybe a Model T? Except it had a wooden back section with several rows of seats added."

"My station hack!" Aunt Gen exclaimed. "Who was driving it?"

"A thin man with a long white beard. The boys called him 'master.' But I think he stole it."

"What makes you think that?" Aunt Gen asked.

"Another man was tied up next to the driver. I didn't get a good look at him but he had white hair and he was wearing a tweed hat. Uh, an Italian-style cap with a cloth brim."

"George," Aunt Gen said. "Darn it!"

"You know him?" Ali asked.

"You do too. He drove you home when you visited my house."

"I'm sorry," Ali said.

"I take it his vehicle can go between worlds?" Mrs. Mishra asked.

"Yes. We were partners when we were younger," Aunt Gen said with a frown.

"Were you a couple?" Ali asked.

"Work partners. George handled transport. It's his specialty. He can take you anywhere. But where do you think *he* is?"

"I don't know," Raahi's mother said. "They brought me in and tied me up with you after that."

"And where are Sie and Raahi?" Ali asked.

Aunt Gen picked up a chair and sat down. "Looking for us, no doubt," she said, "but I think the real question is, *when* are they."

"When?" Ali repeated, puzzled.

Aunt Gen nodded. "Remember when we were spun wildly and it felt like we couldn't breathe?"

"That was awful," Mrs. Mishra said. "Was it some kind of torture, do you think?"

"It was a transport," Aunt Gen said. "We were nowhere for a little while. That's where you go in between somewheres."

"But we didn't go anywhere," Mrs. Mishra pointed out. "We're still in the church."

"True," Aunt Gen said. "Which suggests we moved in time, not space. It got quite dark. It's still dark. So we were transported from day to night. And I would guess we were sent ahead. Sending your enemy back in time is not a good strategy."

"Why not?" Ali asked.

"Well, it would mean that there'd be a second version of the three of us from the future and therefore with foreknowledge. If we managed to free ourselves, we could go find our past selves and warn them."

"So we should go warn ourselves, right?" Ali asked.

"No, dear," Aunt Gen said. "I doubt our enemies would make that mistake."

"So we're in the future," Ali said. "Can we go back?"

"Aside from being illegal, time travel is virtually impossible," Aunt Gen said. "This must have been done with a time spinner from the platinum world. We caught them trying to smuggle platinum artifacts into Egypt years ago and arrested Master Saint-Omer and his associates. I thought we'd destroyed all their otherworld tech, but they must've hidden some."

"What about a reweave?" Ali asked.

"That isn't time travel, but of course it *can* have an impact on the past. You project your consciousness back to a key event on your own timeline and make a small change. But even that is forbidden except in the most extreme circumstances."

"Could you use a reweave to go back and prevent us from being kidnapped?" Mrs. Mishra asked.

"It's too big of a change. Most likely, they'd just kidnap us later in the morning. The bigger the change, the more likely it is to be interwoven with other threads that will pull it back into the existing pattern."

"I don't understand anything you said," Ali admitted.

"The entire direction of events, not just for us but for all the members of the Hunt Club, is based on our being kidnapped and used as hostages. And I assume they're manipulating Silent and Raahi to do something for them, otherwise why hold us? Many people's threads are tangled. We can't change all of them."

"So you can't prevent us from being captured?" Ali asked.

"No. But . . ." Aunt Gen paused to think.

"Do you have an idea?" Mrs. Mishra asked.

Aunt Gen nodded. "Something much more subtle, but it will require a lot of effort. You see, it all goes back to Egypt."

"Egypt?" Ali repeated. "Why?"

"Many years ago, when I was an undercover agent, I discovered that a group was smuggling otherworld artifacts into our world through a portal beneath a pyramid. We think the pharaoh whose pyramid it was had come from a distant world. Anyway, it was long forgotten until Saint-Omer and his gang explored it. They could have gotten enough platinum artifacts from that site to take over our world, but we caught them and destroyed everything they had on them. I was there. With George." She frowned.

"That's *your* timeline," Ali said, "so you can reweave it, right?"

"But subtly," Aunt Gen said. "I have to allow events to roll forward to where we are right now without any disturbance. That's the tricky part."

"You can't just, uh, 'eliminate' Master Saint-Omer?" Ali asked.

"No. Who knows what would happen if I did that. We might not even exist right now. It would change so many timelines."

"What *can* you do?" Ali asked.

"His spinner?" Raahi's mother asked. "Could you break it?"

"Even that would be problematic, because then he couldn't send us to when and where we are now. No, I need to do something that has zero effect *until this very moment*. Something that solves our problem of how to get back but doesn't change anything before now. I still don't know what, but I'm thinking about it. In the meantime, I'm going to close my eyes and see if I can visualize that moment in the cave clearly enough to even *do* a reweave."

* * *

Ali wiggled and squirmed until she'd gotten so close to Mrs. Mishra's taped hands that she could get her teeth on the tape. "Yuck!" she said as she spat out a sticky scrap. "It tastes awful!" But she fought her way through. "Try pulling now," she said.

And it worked! Raahi's mother's hands were free.

It didn't take her long to free her ankles. Then she was on her feet and hurrying to free Aunt Gen. They peeled the tape off their mouths then untaped Ali.

"Allow me," Raahi's mother said, taking hold of one end of the tape on Ali's face.

"Ow! I'll do it," Ali said.

"May I?" Aunt Gen asked, placing a hand over the tape.

"Thanks! Did you dissolve the glue?"

"That's right," Aunt Gen said. "And now I think it's time for introductions. Ali, this is Mrs. Mishra, Raahi's mother. Monali, this is Ali, Silent's best friend from school."

"Pleased to meet you," Mrs. Mishra said with a smile. "Sorry for the circumstances."

"You two don't realize it," Aunt Gen said, "but this is a redo."

"A what?" Raahi's mother asked, surprised.

"Did you reweave?" Ali asked.

"Correct. Because, you see, we are six hours ahead and we need to get back. Master Saint-Omer is hiding us in time. Whoever is trying to find us—most likely Raahi, Silent, and Augie Dorsenhaal—won't be able to because of the temporal shift."

"The what?" Raahi's mother asked.

"I'll show you," Aunt Gen said, reaching into a small pocket in her dress. "This is a platinum-world artifact. It's called a time spinner."

"Master Saint-Omer has one just like it!" Ali exclaimed.

"That's right. So I went all the way back to Egypt, where I'd last seen an artifact like this. We'd smashed several of them to keep them from being misused. However, when I rewove that moment, I saved one. I've kept it all these years, and I sewed a hidden pocket into this dress so that I'd have it on me when I was captured. A thirty-year plan finally coming to fruition," she said with a smile. "Now we'll just . . ." She opened the lid and carefully spun the hands back six hours.

THIRTY-THREE

Reunited

They were standing in the church: Master D, Raahi, and Silent on one side and April, May, and June facing them, with the dappled light from the cracked crusaders' window making colored patches on the floor between them.

"What we need is a strategy," Raahi said.

"True," Sie said. "Does anyone *have* a strategy?"

There was silence.

"We still have what they want," Raahi pointed out.

"And they have three hostages!" Sie snapped. (She didn't know about her aunt's driver.) "But you're right, Raahi. We can still try to do an exchange. Somehow."

"We have a powerful ally here in town," Master D said. "I haven't checked with the local Custodian since we got back, but I'm sure he'll be eager to help. It's funny, now I think of it, that he hasn't shown up already. Usually he monitors magical activity pretty closely."

Sie and Raahi exchanged another of their looks. "Uh, Master D? If anyone who ought to have been in touch *hasn't* been, I'm afraid there's only one explanation," Raahi said.

Master D frowned.

"What are you doing?" Sie demanded. April had begun to dance.

"Spinning my sisters up," April said as she grabbed their hands and all three began to spin around together.

"To hide them?" Raahi asked, but they were already a blur and April did not answer.

Pop. Something shifted and April slowed to a stop. "To protect them when I go with you," she said. "That way we don't have to be divided. Divided is weak, together is strong, right?" She grinned.

Raahi and Silent exchanged a look. "That's true," Sie said.

"Actually, it *is* rather clever," Master D said. "But I take your earlier point about being outnumbered. What with their platinum devices and all those boys, it will be quite hard to—What in the worlds is *that*?"

It sounded like wind howling in a storm, except it was coming from the place where the platform and illusions had been. They backed away and Master D formed a warding with his hands as the air began to flicker.

The sound rose to a high whine. Raahi put his hands over his ears and April and Sie winced.

Something solidified. Three somethings. And there they were: Ali, Aunt Generous, and Monali Mishra.

"Maa!" Raahi cried, running to her at the same time that Sie rushed to give Aunt Gen a hug.

"*I'll* hug *you*," April said, coming over to Ali. "Somebody ought to. Funny customs you Americans have, though," she added as she pulled Ali tightly to her. "Or are you British? I'm having trouble keeping track."

"Who exactly are *you*?" Ali asked somewhat breathlessly as April squeezed her.

"Where did they all come from?" Master D demanded, but everyone was too busy with their greetings to give him an answer.

THIRTY-FOUR

The Master's Study

"Boys!" It was Master Saint-Omer addressing his Hunt Club members, who were once again standing more or less at attention in front of his desk.

"Yes, master," they all said. Except for the two boys who'd been turned into dogs. They barked.

"Who let those dogs in here?"

"They followed us," one of the boys explained.

"Get rid of them! Now, if I may have your attention without any *further* interruptions?" The room fell tensely silent. "I need your reports. Where exactly do we stand?"

The boys exchanged nervous glances. "We still haven't gotten hold of the alien," someone said.

"No, you haven't. Which means?" Saint-Omer demanded.

"Uh, that we haven't completed the mission yet?" another boy said.

"*You* haven't completed *your* assignment!" Saint-Omer exploded, glaring at them. "And what do you propose to do about *that?*"

There was an even longer silence. Finally Rudy cleared his throat and said, "We can still do the exchange, sir, can't we?"

"*Can* we?"

"Uh, you hid the hostages, and the bee aliens are in Boston now, so . . ." Rudy's sentence trailed off.

"So?" Master Saint-Omer repeated, glaring at him.

"So we just have to pick a new place to do the exchange. Uh, somewhere they won't feel like they can fight us."

"And?" Saint-Omer demanded.

"And, uh, well, I guess, be prepared to capture the aliens if they don't cooperate?"

Master Saint-Omer studied Rudy for a tense moment then nodded. "Precisely. A public place with enough people around to prevent them from doing any major workings. It won't prevent *us*, however, because *we* don't care about civilian casualties. We'll bring all our platinum-world tech since those stupid bee-world aliens apparently aren't obeying my orders."

"Why aren't they?" someone asked. "I thought you said their queen ordered them to help us."

"She's lost control of them," Saint-Omer snapped. "Obviously!"

"Yes, sir."

"*We* need their knowledge, but *they* want to use their magic against us. Correct?"

"Yes, master," several boys chorused.

"Which is why I sprayed two of them and why *you* have to make sure the third one gets sprayed!"

"Yes, master."

"Make sure an alien survives, but I don't care what happens to the rest of the group. Is that clear?"

"*Yes, master!*" they chorused, drowning out the barks.

THIRTY-FIVE

Hunting the Hunt Club

Silent, Raahi, Ali, Aunt Gen, and Mrs. Mishra finished hugging each other and started to explain what each group had been doing, until Ali finally interrupted by asking, "Yes, but what should we do now?"

"A very good question, dear," Aunt Gen said. "I don't know about the rest of you, but *my* priority is to find George."

"I still can't reach the Custodian," Master D said.

"What, Henry? Has he gone missing too?" Aunt Gen exclaimed, sounding worried.

"And my watch is going wild," Master D said, frowning and tapping the glass.

"Look! The tracker finally stopped spinning," Sie reported. "I think it was trying to tell us that they were here all along, just not in the same time as us."

"Is there something we can use to track the Hunt Club?" Raahi asked.

"Like this?" April said, holding out her hand. It was a small pocket knife she'd picked up.

"Dropped by one of the boys, most likely," Aunt Gen said. "Put it in the drawer, dear."

Sie did, and soon the tracker needle was spinning again, but it stopped after a few turns and pointed toward the west.

"That's the direction of BAAM," Raahi said. "They probably went back to Master Saint-Omer's study."

"Wait, the needle's turning again," Sie reported. "They must be on the move."

Aunt Gen leaned over to look. "And speeding up. They probably got into a carriage or automobile. Let's wait to see where they stop."

The needle turned past north and swung around until it pointed almost due east.

"Heading downtown," Master D said. "We don't know how far though. Shall we hail a cab?"

"They won't go far," Raahi said. "They want to make it easy for us to find them."

"Do they?" April asked. "Why?"

"Uh, just call it a hunch," Raahi said.

"No, really," April pressed. "Tell me."

"They want *you*," Raahi said. "And your sisters. That's what this is all about, right?"

"My magic." April scowled. "But they won't get it! Not unless they restore my sisters' magic first!"

"Uh, what did you just say?" Sie asked. She'd been talking to Aunt Gen but something about April's comment caught her ear.

"Shouldn't we be going?" Raahi's mother asked.

"April?" Sie persisted. "You're not planning to give them any bee-world magic, right?"

"You should go home," Raahi said, speaking to his mother. "We're about to hunt the hunters, which isn't safe for anyone who can't do magic, Maa."

"And let you go into danger again without me? I don't think so, young man!" she replied.

"We'll all go," Sie said. "We're safer together. Right, April?" she added, giving her a stern look.

April shrugged. "Sure, quiet girl, whatever you say."

And so all six of them (or eight if you knew to count April's spun-up sisters) headed out of the church and walked up Newbury Street toward downtown. When Newbury ended at Arlington, they crossed the street and stepped onto a path that led into the pleasant green lawns and colorful gardens of Boston Common. Up ahead, they could see the rippling blue surface of a large pond where a boat was gliding along. The boat had three rows of benches. In the rear, a large white-painted wooden swan concealed a seat for the driver, who pedaled to spin the propeller.

There was only one passenger on the boat: an older man, hunched over and with his cap pulled down almost over his eyes. Oddly, he was tied round and round with rope and his mouth was taped. The driver of the boat was a young man in a BAAM uniform: Rudy! He was grinning.

Aunt Gen's reaction was surprising. Instead of rushing ahead to rescue George, she slipped behind a clump of lilacs, pulling Raahi's mother with her. "Ali!" she hissed. "Don't let him see you!" And so Ali joined them, leaving Sie, Raahi, April, and Master D standing on the path, puzzled looks on their faces until Sie said, "Of course!"

"Of course what?" Master D asked.

"They think we're still tied up at Emmanuel Church," Aunt Gen explained. "Best not to let them know we escaped."

"Yes, but what about George?" Master D asked.

"I'll conceal us then free him when the swan boat circles back this way," Aunt Gen said from behind the bush. "We'll do it at the far end of the pond where the bushes are thick to avoid anyone else from the Hunt Club noticing. The rest of you should keep going until you find Saint-Omer. As soon as we free George, we'll follow you."

"You can all wait here while *I* find him," April said. "And make him restore my sisters' magic!" She looked very grim and determined.

"Remember what you said about not being divided," Raahi reminded her.

"I like you, boy, but you're terrible in a fight."

Raahi opened his mouth—and closed it again. He couldn't really disagree with her about that.

"Why do you think Rudy is paddling around in plain sight with George?" Master D asked.

"They're making a show of him," Raahi said. "It's almost a taunt, isn't it?"

"To lure us further into the park," Sie added. "It's crowded today. I suppose they think we'll be unwilling to risk hurting bystanders, which is true. But I bet the park will clear out as soon as we start dueling. Master D, are you going first?"

"Well, I suppose so," he said, sounding reluctant.

And so Raahi, Silent, and April headed down the path with Master D in front of them, leaving the escaped hostages hiding in the bushes.

The pond came into fuller view ahead of them with the long footbridge arching over it. They turned and followed the path alongside the water until it branched, the right side leading to the bridge. "Which way?" Raahi asked. "Over the pond, do you think, or toward the statue of George Washington?" There was a large statue off to their left, surrounded by a flower garden.

"Statue of *who*?" Silent asked.

"There," Raahi said, pointing. "No, wait, that doesn't look right." Instead of a bronze man on a horse holding a sword, there was a bronze woman on a horse holding a rose and a sword.

"The statue of President Abigail Adams?" Sie asked.

"But that's supposed to be—wait, who was the first president of the United States in the side door world?" Raahi demanded.

"George Washington," Silent said. "Abigail Adams was the second president. She'd been vice president under Washington. How is this going to help us find Saint-Omer?"

"No, her husband, John Adams, was the second president." Raahi frowned. "Wait, this might be one of those differences between worlds. Have you had woman presidents in the side door world?"

"Of course! Women sorcerers are so important," Sie said. "Adams used her magic to help Washington win the Revolutionary War. I thought you were an expert on history."

"I guess not," Raahi said.

"Our enemies have arrived," Master D announced. "They're on the far side of the bridge. April, get behind us, please."

It was Master Saint-Omer and a group of young men from BAAM, along with two dogs. They stopped on the far side of the long footbridge, on the other side of the pond.

"I want the aliens!" Saint-Omer said, raising his voice to reach them.

Before the others could react, April stepped forward and called back. "*I* want the counter!"

"Counter?" Saint-Omer repeated, sounding puzzled. "What's the alien talking about?"

"To cure my sisters!"

"Uh, April?" Sie said. "Where are you going?"

"I'll deal with him," April hissed, her eyes flashing angrily. "You can have whatever's left," she added as she headed up the path to the bridge. "I *might* spare your life!" she said in a loud voice to Saint-Omer. "But only if you give my sisters their magic back!"

"April, wait!" Raahi called.

"Oh dear," Master D said.

Saint-Omer gestured toward a tree that leaned out over the water by the base of the bridge. *Crrr-ack!* Its trunk broken, it began to fall toward April.

Sie spoke the words of a wind-weaving and blew it aside so that its crown splashed into the pond, scattering indignant ducks and scaring picnickers away.

April ignored the tree. She was already on the bridge by the time Sie caught up with her and grabbed her arm. But with the strength of three, April shrugged her off and kept going.

A whoosh of water spouted up from the pond and rose above them, then with a loud *craaaack* turned into a huge chunk of jagged ice whistling downward toward April and Sie. Raahi and Master D both gasped; Sie shouted a redirection. The ice veered toward shore and smashed down on a flower bed.

April stopped walking and turned to stare at the ice. Her eyes narrowed. "His ice crushed flowers and bees. That was bad!" But it was difficult to hear the last few words because something was buzzing loudly.

It was thousands of bees. They came from all directions, aiming for the Hunt Club. Saint-Omer cursed, the boys began dancing and waving and slapping, and the dogs howled.

"He shouldn't have done that," April said. "And *you* shouldn't have redirected it at a garden, girl!"

"Just listen for a second," Sie said. "I have a plan."

"I don't need a plan! Now that I don't have to take directs, I can do whatever I want," April said, striding ahead again.

"Then try doing something smart," Sie said as she hurried to catch up. "Not just the first thing that pops into your head."

"What's wrong with . . . Oh. Actually, that makes sense," April said, pausing to let Sie catch up. "Maybe I'll try thinking first." Then she turned to eye Saint-Omer and his Hunt Club and her expression became angry again. "Or maybe I'll let those bees sting them until they're *dead!*"

Raahi and Master D were hurrying to join April and Sie. "Do you mean to tell me," Raahi said as they approached, "that Saint-Omer reached out to a queen bee from a bee world and arranged to steal bee magic, all without preparing even one defense against being *stung* by bees?"

"Apparently," Sie said as Raahi came up beside her. "But you should call the bees off, April. We still need to get information out of Saint-Omer."

"I like the way they're screaming," she said. "But I guess you're right." She shrugged and waved her hand. The cloud of insects buzzed up, hovering menacingly over the Hunt Club members.

Saint-Omer recovered first and began to shout cures—although the magical first aid seemed unable to get rid of the red spots, which the boys kept touching as if they were a source of considerable irritation. "That was stupid, alien!" he snapped. "But an impressive demonstration," he added, looking thoughtful. "You'll give me that magic too. The ability to turn the entire insect world against my enemies will prove useful. All right, here's what we're going to do. The rest of you, back away and let the alien come to me! I'll cure the alien's sisters but only if everyone does *exactly* what I say."

"How can we possibly trust him?" Raahi demanded.

"I agree," Master D said. "Obviously he's highly unrelia—"

"What do you want?" April called, ignoring Raahi and Master D.

"I need you on the far side of the pond so we can speak in private," Saint-Omer said. "I just have a few questions about your world's magic. That's all. My boy will ferry you over in the boat."

"Don't do it," Raahi warned.

"Why can't I just walk across the bridge?" April demanded. "Are you afraid? Because you should be!"

"Cautious, shall we say?" Saint-Omer said. "My boy will secure your hands so you don't pull any more magical stunts."

April shook her head. "I don't think so! Tell me the cure for my sisters."

"Once you've done what *I* want," Saint-Omer insisted, "we'll talk about what you want. And where exactly are your sisters?"

"Tell me how to cure them," April said. "You don't need to talk to them, just me."

"Very well," Saint-Omer said. "As long as I can talk to one of you."

"If I may suggest a tactical retreat?" Master D said. "We can discuss his offer where we're not as easy for him to reach with falling trees and giant blocks of ice."

"Stay out of this, over," April snapped. She was just turning back toward Master Saint-Omer and his Hunt Club members when Sie leaned close and whispered something in her ear.

April paused, considering, then nodded before turning to speak to Saint-Omer. "Okay, I'll go in your stupid boat with your stupid boy," she announced.

"What?" Raahi exclaimed. "Did I miss something?"

"Shh," Sie warned.

"I guess I did," he muttered as Rudy steered the swan boat toward the bank and April hurried back down the lawn to meet it.

There was a low stone wall separating the lawn from the water. Rudy pulled the boat up beside it. "Get in, alien," he said, looking smug. He was holding a coil of rope.

"Uh, Silent? If she sets foot on his boat, we've lost control of the situation," Master D whispered. "Do you think you could do something to stop her? As in *right now*?"

"I don't think so," Sie said.

"What an ungovernable child!" Master D grumbled as April approached the boat.

The glances April and Sie shot Master D made it abundantly clear that neither appreciated his comment, even though it wasn't clear which of them he meant. Perhaps both.

THIRTY-SIX

Losing April

Saint-Omer smiled as April approached the swan boat. "That's right, alien! Now my boy will tie you up and bring you to the dock, where I will take possession of you. As for the rest of you . . ." He was addressing Sie, Raahi, and Master D, who had followed April and were standing near the base of the bridge, at the edge of the pond. (Of course Aunt Gen, Ali, and Mrs. Mishra were still hiding somewhere out of sight.) "If the alien doesn't cooperate fully, I'll kill you one by one!" Saint-Omer said, taking something out of his pocket. It was a small platinum-colored pistol. "I believe a demonstration might ensure that you take my threat as seriously as it's intended," he added as he raised the pistol and took aim.

"Wards," Sie hissed as Raahi stepped behind Master D—and just in time, it seemed, when a *pop* from the little gun was followed by a *whizzzz* as a tiny platinum bead came speeding toward them.

"Oh dear," Master D said as it splatted into the palm of the hand he had raised to form a ward-sign. The hand became metallic. So did his arm. The sheen of metal spread from there, taking over so quickly that neither Raahi nor Sie could react. And then he was a statue standing on the lawn beside the pond, his face frozen in a platinum expression of alarm.

"Since you've never been to the Platinum World, it's fair to assume you don't know a ward against this magic," Saint-Omer said. "And it's also fair to assume that I'll use it on the rest of you if the alien gives me even the slightest trouble!"

April glanced at Sie, who nodded.

Then April stepped aboard the swan boat.

"Do something!" Raahi hissed.

"Have you read about telepathosis?" Sie asked in a whisper.

"Sensing other people's thoughts?"

"And planting them. It takes years of training, but it *is* possible to push a detailed thought to someone else."

"Who were you sending thoughts to?" Raahi whispered.

"You'll see," Sie whispered back.

April was already on the boat and Rudy was tying her hands together. He tore a piece of tape, pressed it over her mouth, and pointed for her to sit on the bench behind George. Then he began to pedal the boat across the pond.

But before he got very far, the boat turned left, heading for the bridge.

"Take her to the dock!" Master Saint-Omer shouted, waving him away.

But the swan boat accelerated, kicking up a frothy white bow wave as it headed straight for the bridge as if aiming to go under it. "It's not me!" Rudy complained, trying to turn the boat. "Something's gone wrong with it!"

The bow of the boat slipped beneath the bridge, and the boys hurried to the far side to lean over and look for it to come out.

There was a tense moment as everyone waited for it to appear.

It didn't.

Chaos erupted on the bridge as dogs barked, boys rushed back and forth to lean over the railings, and Saint-Omer shouted at them.

When it became apparent that the boat was truly gone, Silent cleared her throat. "Now *you* will listen to *me*," she said. "I've hidden the bee girl and you won't find her unless you do *exactly* what I—"

"Just a minute!" Saint-Omer interrupted. "I still have your loved ones and you'll never see them again unless . . . unless . . ." He seemed to deflate as Aunt Gen and Mrs. Mishra came out from behind a bush beside the onramp to the bridge, where they stood facing Saint-Omer.

"You were saying?" Sie asked.

"What do you want?" Saint-Omer snapped.

"Your spray cans," Sie said. "I see some of the boys are holding them."

"We're *not* going to give you our alien tech!" Saint-Omer growled, raising his platinum gun again.

"Uh, Sie?" Raahi said as Saint-Omer took aim.

"May I introduce myself?" Raahi's mother announced, stepping forward. "I am Mrs. Mishra, and I must say, I'm *very* upset by your conduct as one of the instructors at my son's new school. You're setting an *extremely* poor example for these boys, so I'm afraid I've had to take the liberty of disabling that little toy gun of yours." She began to walk toward him on the bridge.

"Maa!" Raahi cried from down on the lawn beside the bridge. "Don't!" And then Raahi and Sie were running toward the bridge. But they were too far away to prevent what happened next.

"Thank you for providing such a convenient target," Saint-Omer said with an evil smile as Mrs. Mishra approached him. *Pop.* A platinum bead came whizzing toward her.

"Wait," Aunt Gen said, holding out a hand to stop Raahi, who had raced ahead of Sie on the path to the bridge. "She'll be all right."

The platinum bead splatted onto Mrs. Mishra's dress and spread out. She glanced down and frowned. "Not only are you are very bad instructor, you're also *terribly* impolite to parents. This stain will probably not come out, even with dry cleaning. And weren't you listening when I told you your gun no longer works?"

He raised it and shot her again. ***Pop. Zzzzzzzp. Splat.***

Her eyebrows rose. "Now you'll have to purchase me a new dress, sir. Assuming you're not in some magical prison or worse, of course."

He stared at the gun in his hand. "How did you . . ."

"*That* is for *me* to know," Mrs. Mishra said. "All *you* need to know is that platinum magic will no longer bother us."

"And you're surrounded," added a voice from the far side of the bridge. It was Master Sontheil, along with the principal of Linacre College and a dozen more masters. "We've just come from the Boston Public Library where the young man you left to guard the door is, well, where is he? Oh, there he goes," she added as a lanky, red-brown spaniel came rushing onto the bridge and began to sniff the other dogs.

"Did you send for them, Sie?" Raahi asked.

"I asked Aunt Gen to. And I communicated with her about George and the boat. I told her to have Ali steer it. Then I sent instructions to Ali and your mother."

"I thought Rudy was driving the boat," Raahi said. "It sounded just like him."

"An illusion. It was Ali. Rudy's taped up in the bushes over there." Sie pointed to the right where the pond went around a corner. "And Ali and George took the boat into the modern world to hide April and her sisters. Aunt Gen and I arranged it." She smiled.

"Nice! But why," Raahi asked her, "didn't the gun turn my mother into a statue?"

"Because," Silent whispered back, taking care that Master Saint-Omer didn't hear, "it works by hijacking your own magic and using it to turn you into metal, and she doesn't have any magic. But she sure is good at bluffing. I thought she might be."

"Clever! What's going to happen now?" Raahi asked.

"Good question," Sie said, then she stepped forward to stand beside Raahi's mother. "Saint-Omer!" she called. "You can't win! Put your gun down or you'll all be turned to dogs. What do you think, Mrs. Mishra? Mangy, flea-covered mutts?"

"Skunks would serve them right but I don't want to have to smell them, so let's go with dogs. *Old* dogs. Lame and beginning to lose their hair."

Saint-Omer looked extremely annoyed. "See here," he snapped. "You don't actually think I'm going to—"

Fwoosh. Another young man turned into a dog. Sie raised an eyebrow. "Who's next?" she asked.

"All right, all right!" Saint-Omer grumbled, placing the gun at his feet and raising his hands.

"Hunt Club members," Sie called. "Don't put those spray cans down yet. You're going to spray each other and your master with them. Oh, and make sure Saint-Omer swallows some of it too!"

"No!" Saint-Omer cried as a half dozen spray cans were aimed at him. "Stop that!" But they seemed quite eager to wet him down with the spray. Even the dogs were excited to get in on the action, barking and growling as he was sprayed.

"That's enough," Sie called. "Don't use it all. You have to spray yourselves too. *And* the dogs."

The Hunt Club members turned their spray cans on each other and kept spraying until they ran out.

"You boys ought to be ashamed of yourselves!" Mrs. Mishra scolded. "I hope you're all expelled. I certainly don't approve of my son having to be in the same school as you."

They looked tongue-tied and hangdog now, standing in their damp blazers on the bridge with their wet hair sticking to their foreheads as antimagic compound dripped down them.

"What should we do with Saint-Omer?" Raahi asked. But the Linacre masters were already surrounding him. One of them picked up a roll of tape that the Hunt Club boys had dropped and began to tape his wrists together while another held him firmly by the collar.

"Make sure he can't escape," Aunt Gen said.

The principal nodded grimly and replied, "Don't worry about that."

"Auntie, I think it's safe for them to come back now," Sie said, and Aunt Gen nodded and waved her white handkerchief in the air.

The swan boat came out from under the bridge. George was in the rear seat, pedaling. Ali, April, May, and June were looking like tourists as they licked brightly colored popsicles. George had hidden them in the modern world until Aunt Gen called him back.

The Hunt Club boys hung over the bridge rail, mouths open in surprise, as George steered the swan boat to the bank and everyone got out.

Ali, April, May, and June stepped off the boat, smiling and licking their popsicles. "You got him!" April exclaimed. "Good!" But their smiles turned to expressions of alarm as the Linacre masters began to lead Saint-Omer away.

"Where are they taking him?" April exclaimed.

"We're taking him back to Oxford for questioning," the principal said as the Linacre masters pushed Saint-Omer down the far side of the bridge.

Then the masters paused for a moment as Master Sontheil turned and waved. "I'm so sorry about Augie, but we'll research cures for being platinumized when we get back. It's amazing, really, that there weren't more casualties. Good work, Silent and Raahi," she added. "Please come visit us on your next break. We'll be in touch with your headmasters to let them know we're saving spots for you at Oxford when you're ready. Oh, and the bee girls are welcome anytime. In fact, they can come with us now if they like. Our gardens could use their attention, and—"

"Hey!" April exclaimed. "Not so fast!"

"Get him back, sister!" May said.

"Make him fix our magic!" June added.

April was already forming runes with her hands. May and June moved between April and Sie, who was saying, "Wait, April, you don't have to . . ."

It was too late. April was levitating Saint-Omer up, legs flailing uselessly. He zoomed away from the Linacre masters and over the pond. It looked like she planned to land him on the grassy bank beside her. However . . .

"Stop that!" the principal of Linacre College cried, pointing at Saint-Omer, whose flight stopped above the middle of the pond, caught between his pull and April's.

A tug of war ensued with Saint-Omer cursing and shouting for them to put him down while April and the principal scowled and gestured.

And then April leaned back and gestured so strongly toward her side that Saint-Omer jerked forward, free of the principal's magical pull. But instead of landing on the lawn, he splashed down in the pond and disappeared beneath the surface.

The mallard ducks that had been swimming nearby quacked loudly, but when he did not resurface, they went back about their business.

"Uh, April? He's got his hands taped together," Raahi pointed out. "I doubt he can swim."

"Serves him right!" April snapped.

"But what about our magic?" June asked.

"That's right, sister," May added. "Don't drown him until he restores our powers."

"I'd like mine back too," Ali said.

Sie, who was up on the bridge with Raahi, Aunt Gen, and Mrs. Mishra, muttered a working.

Whooooosh! Up came the soaking wet Saint-Omer, sputtering and coughing. He sluiced across the pond, scattering indignant ducks as his heels kicked up waves. It looked like he was being dragged backward by his collar. With a wave of her hand, Sie deposited him on the lawn at April, May, and June's feet, near where the platinum statue of Master D stood. "See what he knows," she said.

"Now see here, children!" the Linacre principal exclaimed, looking even more indignant than the ducks. "He's our prisoner and I demand you return him at once!"

"Put a sock in it, Ralph," Master Sontheil said. "My sympathy is entirely with the girls and yours should be too! Let them see if they can find out how to undo the effects of the spray, for goodness sake."

"Well now, I say, this is *highly* irregular, Ursula," the principal grumbled. "But I suppose we can give them a minute or two."

"I'm going to turn that pompous over into a pincushion for bees!" April snapped.

Sie, who had hurried off the bridge and around the edge of the pond to join the other girls, said, "Just ignore him. You've got your chance."

"Tell me how to take it off!" April demanded, leaning over the very damp Saint-Omer where he lay on his back on the lawn, his arms taped, blinking water out of his eyes.

"Uh . . ."

"Uh *what!*" April shouted.

"Uh, well, actually, I can't help you. It may lessen over time, but that's not a certainty."

"Can we kick him, sister?" June asked as May gave him an exploratory tap with her toe.

"Ow!" he howled.

"That was nothing," May said. "I'm *really* going to kick you if you don't—"

"Wait. I'll put a compulsion on him," Sie said. "A really strong one. He'll tell you everything he knows."

"Do it," April said.

*"**Veritatem semper et tantum!***" Sie cried, her voice ringing with power.

"I am a very bad man and I confess I still want to take over the world," Saint-Omer said, even though no one had asked him a question yet. "But now I probably can't, and that makes me very angry."

"I hated that stupid beehive hairstyle," June admitted—again without any prompting.

"Me too," May added.

"I felt bad about tricking you and the good-looking boy," April said, then her eyes grew wide. "Oops. That really *is* a powerful spell, silent girl."

"I forgot to clean my dentures this morning," the principal of Linacre College admitted to his colleagues over on the far side of the bridge—then hurried to clap his hand over his mouth before he said anything more.

"I must confess," Raahi announced, "that I had *quite* the crush on Silent Lee when I first met her. But now we're best friends and I only have a small crush on her," he said—then clapped his hand over his mouth too.

Aunt Gen and Mrs. Mishra had come more slowly and were just joining them on the lawn. "It's been difficult raising Raahi here without his father but we still hold out hope that he may be able to get a visa," Mrs. Mishra announced. "Goodness me, why in the world did I say that?"

Aunt Gen patted her reassuringly. "It was Sie's truth compulsion. It's so powerful, it's affecting everyone. It'll probably have a *permanent* effect on Saint-Omer."

"Sounds like a good idea for someone as dishonest as him," Sie snapped, scowling down at the wet master. Then she paused and eyed Aunt Gen. "Who's my real mother?" she demanded.

"I, I . . . uh . . . am . . . amazed at how strong you're becoming!" Aunt Gen said, struggling to change the topic.

Sie's eyebrow rose. "I guess I should've asked you sooner when the compulsion was having its strongest affect." She shrugged then leaned over the wet man with the stringy beard. "As for you, Saint-Omer," she hissed, her eyes narrowing as he squirmed at her feet. "You will answer all of April's questions with *complete honesty!*"

"Wh-what are they going to do with me?"

"Don't speak unless you're asked a question," Aunt Gen instructed. "All right, ask away, girls."

"Do you want me to kick you again?" May demanded.

"No!"

"Ask him about the spray," Sie said.

April leaned over him. "Tell us the counter to that spray!"

"I, I can't," he said, his voice trembling as he braced for another kick.

April waved a hand and a buzzing cloud of bees assembled beside her. "I'll have them start stinging you unless you tell me."

"He really can't," Sie said.

"Why not?" April demanded, looking at Sie in surprise.

"I don't know, but if he says he can't, he can't. He has to tell the truth."

"Darn! All right, Mister Master, *why* can't you tell us the cure?"

"I don't know it. No one does. No one in this world at least. That's the point of alien magic. It can't be countered."

"Then you're useless!" April cried as her sisters began to sniff like they were going to cry. "I *will* let the bees sting you to death!"

"Uh, April? Why don't you let them take him to Oxford now?" Sie said. "Maybe they'll figure out where he got the platinum tech. It might be possible to get in touch with that world and find out what the counter is, but only if you give them a chance to interrogate him. They're probably experts at this kind of thing."

"Actually, we are," Master Sontheil said. "And I promise we'll research the matter thoroughly." She glanced at the platinum statue of Master Dorsenhaal as she said this. A pigeon had landed on his shoulder.

April turned to May and June. "What do you say, sisters?"

They frowned. "Whatever you say, April," May said, and June nodded.

"All right, quiet girl, we'll let them take him to their Oxford hive. But *we're* going to stay here and search *his* hive," April said.

"We don't live in a hive and neither did he," the principal of Linacre College said, sounding very superior.

"Of course he did!" April said. "Everyone does."

"Aunt Gen?" Sie asked. "Shall we go to Saint-Omer's study?"

"It's a good idea," Aunt Gen agreed. "As April has no doubt deduced, there might be a clue there as to how to undo the damage to her sisters."

"And how to un-statue Master D?" Raahi asked.

"I hope so," Aunt Gen said.

"Are you also looking for clues about the Custodian?" Sie asked. "Who you seem to be on a first name basis with? Is it Harold?"

"That's right, dear." Aunt Gen frowned.

"This way," George announced. He'd stepped out of the swan boat and was pointing toward Arlington Street. "My hack's parked nearby."

"Oh, Raahi!" Mrs. Mishra exclaimed as soon as the Linacre Masters and their prisoners were out of sight. "An invitation to go to college at Oxford! I'm so proud of you, and it's only your first week of high school! But I *do* hope the rest of the instructors are better than that one was."

"I think they will be, Maa. It wouldn't be difficult."

"What will they do with him?" Mrs. Mishra asked.

Aunt Gen pursed her lips. "Probably send him through the multidoor to some uninhabited world," she said. "Come on. Let's follow George, everyone."

"What about those dreadful boys?" Mrs. Mishra asked. "Shouldn't someone speak to their parents?"

"When we get to BAAM, we'll let them know what happened," Aunt Gen said.

And then they were hurrying past the statue of President Adams and along the path to where the Model T station hack awaited them.

Sie frowned when she saw it. In the past, she was certain it had just two rows of benches. Now there were four. *Maybe,* she thought, *it adjusts as needed.*

Soon everyone was seated and George was in his proper place at the wheel as they *putt-putted* down Commonwealth Ave. The sun was warm and the traffic light, with only a few horse-drawn carriages *clop-clopping* along. It was a lovely autumn day in turn-of-the-century magical Boston. The only odd thing about it was the fact that Boston Common, with its many picnic spots and pleasant gardens, was almost entirely devoid of people—but a magical duel in the middle of a crowded park does tend to send people running.

THIRTY-SEVEN

Cleaning Up

George waited by his vehicle in front of the Boy's Academy of Alchemy and Magic while April and her sisters, along with Silent, Raahi, Ali, Mrs. Mishra, and Aunt Gen, went to the rear of the big brick building. The door to Master Saint-Omer's chambers was marked with a small brass plaque bearing his name, quite shiny and new compared to the names on the neighboring doors.

Aunt Gen glanced at Sie, who said, "Stand back," and sent such a powerful *whoosh* of wind at the door that it crashed inward and landed flat on the carpet with a thump. "Sorry," she said, "but he'd put wards on the lock."

"I'll fix it, don't worry," Aunt Gen said. Then she did a double take. "Are you *sure* he just started here?" she exclaimed. "There's so much *stuff.*" The room was strangely crowded with piles of old books and unusual-looking magical instruments.

"Darn! He hasn't unpacked all his boxes," Raahi complained after tripping on one. "I'll go through books," he added, getting to his feet and heading for the crowded shelves.

"Help me with his artifacts and devices, my dear," Aunt Gen said, and Sie nodded and began to gather them. They pushed papers aside to make room on the desk for their growing pile.

"Here," Raahi's mother said, working to clear more space on the desk.

"Where did he get all these?" Sie asked. "His collection must be worth a fortune!"

"Stolen, I imagine," Aunt Gen said.

"The books are definitely stolen," Raahi said. "They've got book plates from different colleges, uh, mostly Linacre. Did he go there?"

"Expelled," Aunt Gen said.

"Then how did he get a job teaching?" Mrs. Mishra exclaimed.

"Linacre's records are sealed," Aunt Gen said, "because the graduates do secret work, which means it might be difficult to verify someone's diploma."

"These books are by people who've visited other worlds," Raahi said. "Did you know," he added, flipping through a leather-bound volume, "that there's a world in which birds are highly magical and sorcerers collect their feathers? Hmm, I wonder if this feather is . . ." He waved it toward them.

"Raahi!" Sie shouted. "Stop that!" The instruments had lifted off the desk and begun to float upward, but they fell back when Raahi clapped the book shut on the feather.

"Sorry," he said.

"Look for anything to do with platinum," Aunt Gen said, "but stay away from other topics, if you don't mind."

Ali came out of the bedroom holding a small wooden chest. "This is locked," she said. "What should I do with it?"

"Probably his personal papers," Aunt Gen suggested. "It's about the right size for that. Put it down, dear, and we'll try to open it once we finish searching the rooms."

April came out of the kitchen with a large jar of honey and a spoon, which she was licking. May and June were still in the kitchen. They'd gotten into honey too. "He has dozens of jars!" April exclaimed, sounding pleased. "I guess he wasn't *all* bad."

Raahi chuckled.

"What's so funny, boy?" April demanded.

"Well . . . he stockpiled honey because he was going to force you to work for him," Raahi explained. "It was to feed his captives."

"Then he *was* all bad," April said. "But at least the honey's good. Have you found the cures for your over and my sisters?"

Raahi frowned.

"Not yet," Sie said. "But we will. I hope. Do you want to help?"

"Keep looking," April said, heading back to the kitchen to eat more honey with her sisters.

They were beginning to get discouraged when someone knocked on the door (Aunt Gen having magicked it back into place).

"I wonder if George is coming to check up on us?" Aunt Gen said.

"I'll get it," Sie said. "Stay back."

"Be careful!" Raahi warned.

Sie swung the door open.

It was a tall, dignified man, very dark in complexion and dressed in an elegant gray suit with a narrow silk tie beneath a colorful vest consisting of vertical stripes in alternating red and orange—the colors of the school. He was also wearing a bowler hat, dark gray like his suit, and a silver monocle. The collar of his white shirt was high, and he held himself stiffly upright as he looked down at Sie. "Young woman," he said rather sternly, "what do you think you're doing here?"

"Are you . . .?" Sie paused, not quite sure who he was.

"The headmaster. Yes." He noticed that there were more people behind Sie and an eyebrow rose in question.

"You'd better come in," Sie said, stepping back.

"Instead of your leaving?" he asked.

"Something like that," she said.

"How about instead of the *entire city* becoming aware of the most *dreadful* and *inappropriate* of scandals?" Aunt Gen said, coming over to stand beside Sie.

"Generous Lee? What in the world are *you* doing here?" He came in, swinging the door behind him and taking off his hat, but he seemed puzzled by the lack of any place clean enough to set it down.

"I'll just put it on top of this pile of stolen instruments," Sie offered, taking it from him.

Raahi, who was still over by the bookshelves, looked at the headmaster guiltily.

"You're one of our new students!" the headmaster exclaimed. "Why are you going through Master Saint-Omer's books—and where *is* he? He missed his classes today, as did a dozen of his students."

Aunt Gen slipped a hand behind his arm and drew him toward the door leading into the bedroom. "Ali," she said, "I think you've done enough searching in here. Why don't you help Sie and Raahi go through the books? The headmaster and I need to have a conversation."

Mrs. Mishra cleared her throat.

"And I'm sure he'd like to meet Raahi's mother," Aunt Gen added, holding the door for Mrs. Mishra to join them.

"All right," Sie said, "has anyone found *anything* to do with platinum magic?"

"I found more honey," April called from the kitchen. "I think it's helping my sisters. The smart boy is finding a cure for them soon, right?"

"Uh, right," Sie replied, glancing at Raahi where he was still going through books.

"No luck here," he said. He'd gone through most of the books already. "Sorry."

"Nothing in the bedroom?" Sie asked.

Ali shook her head. "But that box I found is kind of interesting," she added. "Too bad it's locked."

"Let's see." Sie leaned over it. "Five tumblers. Combination lock. Not warded. Should be easy enough to figure out with a well-controlled wind-weaving. Hold on." She let her eyelids flutter closed and reached out to gather five small puffs of air. They swished inside the lock and down into the openings where each tumbler was supposed to go when set to the right number. "I see the pattern," she said. And then she spun the numbered dials.

Click.

"Careful," Ali said. "It might be a trap."

"Explosives?" Raahi asked.

"Or a deadly curse," Ali suggested.

"We won't know until we open it," Sie pointed out as she lifted the lid.

The only thing in the box was a velvet bag. Sie picked it up, loosened the tie, and let the contents slip out. It was an elegant, valuable-looking antique necklace in the form of two dragons, one in shiny silver (or was it platinum!), the other in bluish steel. They were biting each other's tails.

"Try it on," Ali said.

"I don't think it's jewelry," Sie said, frowning.

"Then what is it?" Ali asked.

"It looks like a reference to strange loop theory," Raahi said, coming over. "An endless loop, right? But that's usually symbolized with a single snake or dragon chasing it tail, not two. Huh." He picked it up and brought it to the nearest window for more light. "The eyes are very realistic," he said. "They even seem to be moving—like the Mona Lisa."

"You're not serious, are you?" Sie asked.

"Leonardo da Vinci's masterpiece? Yes. People who've been to the Louvre say that the eyes follow you. It's an illusion, of course." He frowned. "But these eyes really *are* moving."

"You'd better put it back," Ali said.

"It's getting bigger now," Raahi exclaimed. "Hey!" He dropped it. "It's starting to move!"

It was considerably larger, and there were hissing sounds coming from it.

"Looks like we finally found some platinum-world magic," Sie said.

"Dragons?" April asked, sticking her head in from the kitchen. "I've run into them on my explorations. They eat people."

The dragons were very alive and getting larger. They began to chase each other, knocking over side tables and clearing the shelves of books with their wild thrashing.

The bedroom door opened and for a few seconds Sie could see her aunt, Raahi's mother and the headmaster staring out at the writhing dragons.

Then the headmaster slammed the door shut—and just in time. The platinum dragon had lunged at them.

It was very loud and dangerous in the main room. Sie, Ali, and Raahi backed into the kitchen, where they took refuge with April, May, and June.

"They're destroying the instruments and books!" Raahi complained.

"I'm trying all sorts of wards and blocks, but nothing seems to work on them," Sie said. "I can't even get into their heads to do an influence. Look out!" A long, scaly tail had just smacked the kitchen doorframe, shaking the wall so hard that several jars of honey fell and broke.

Then the dragons leapt at each other and fell hard on the desk, smashing the wooden box from which they'd come—and, incidentally, flattening the headmaster's bowler too.

As soon as the box splintered, the dragons stopped fighting and crouched, hissing. Then they began to shrink again but not all the way back to the size of the necklace. The shrinking stopped when they were about six feet long. And then other changes began to happen. Horns and fangs receded, tails shrank, rear legs elongated, and they stood up. There, standing side by side, were two men.

One was very unusual in appearance. His skin was platinum in color, and his long robe and high boots were metallic too. He had silver eyebrows and a high forehead, and his hair fell in silvery waves down his back. Only his eyes were a different color: a warm gold.

The other was the Custodian from the Boston Public Library. Sie and Raahi recognized him at once. He was wearing a tweed suit as usual and he had the same coffee-colored complexion and neat, kinky short hair. However, the book he always carried under one arm and his gold-rimmed glasses were both missing.

"Harold!" Aunt Gen exclaimed from the bedroom doorway. "Are you all right?"

"Ah, Generous," he said. "I'm glad *you're* all right, and I see you've reconnected with your daughter."

"Niece," Gen corrected.

"Of course. Forgive me. I'm a little stunned, I must confess. Where is Saint-Omer? I was dueling with him when this gentleman leapt at me in dragon form." He gestured toward the other man.

"Yours is a powerful dragon," the platinum man said. His English was good but he spoke with a thick accent and slowly, as if he were far from home. "Sorry to fight you, but it wasn't my choice. The magic of that box is overwhelming. I *had* to follow that annoying man's commands. I tried to smash the box but I couldn't, not on purpose anyway. It's lucky we fell on it by accident. Are you all right?"

"I'm fine. Thank you for asking."

"Where is our captor now?" the platinum man asked.

"Don't worry," Aunt Gen said. "We're dealing very firmly with him."

The man nodded. "Good! He stole many weapons, and when I tried to stop him, he used the box on me. It's an extremely powerful device from our Museum of Ancient Sorcery, where I am one of the curators."

"Do you have hostile intentions toward our world?" the Custodian asked.

"Of course not. We are peaceful people," the man replied. "Hundreds of years ago, our ancestors invaded other worlds, but we have long since evolved beyond such primitive hostilities and we only keep a small number of weapons, locked up in a museum, to remind us not to repeat that terrible period of history again. I assure you, my only wish is to go home."

The Custodian nodded. "Very well. Do you need to go through Egypt?"

"Through our old portal, yes, but do not put yourselves to any inconvenience. It is but a day's flight in dragon form." And then he began to shimmer.

"Wait!" Sie called. "Can you help us? One of our friends was turned to metal, and these girls lost their magic."

He firmed up again and turned to study Sie. "I had no idea," he said, his silvery eyebrows rising.

"Uh, did you understand my question?" Sie asked.

"Yes, but I did not expect to encounter such a powerful sorcerer, and so young! There are so few in any of the populated worlds with your potential, if I may say—"

"I'd rather you not," Aunt Gen interrupted quite firmly. "But it *would* be helpful if you'd offer your advice about our friend who was turned to platinum."

"That's regrettable. Show me."

"And my sisters?" April added, coming out of the kitchen.

"I'll see if there's anything I can do. Please take me to the statue at once. That effect is irreversible if it sets in fully."

And so, with the headmaster leading, they walked right through the school with everyone coming out of their classrooms to stare at them— especially at the platinum man, but also at the triplets, who, when they realized they were the center of attention, began to wave and smile like royalty.

When their group reached the street, yet another row of seating had appeared, so they all climbed into the station hack and were quite comfortable as it *putt-putted* back to Boston Common, where George parked and they climbed out.

The new statue had attracted a circle of puzzled citizens.

"Is it someone famous?" a bystander asked.

"Excuse me," Harold (the Custodian) said. "I suggest you step back."

The crowd of spectators grew in size as the platinum sorcerer strode over to the statue and began to hum. It was deep and resonant and musical. He had a lovely voice. Soon he began to sing, although not in any language they could understand. His singing grew in volume until finally he hit a long note that seemed to be the perfect landing place for the melody. And then he stopped. And Master D, no longer made of metal, smiled and said, "Lovely! I enjoyed that very much. And if I'm not mistaken, my magic is unblocked now too!"

The crowd applauded, and Sie, Raahi, and the bee girls rushed to Master D and hugged him. "There, there," he kept saying. "I'm all right, really!"

"I wish *I* could be fixed," Ali said sadly, but no one was paying attention to her. "I used to be able to do workings," she added, addressing Mrs. Mishra, who was standing nearby. "Until they sprayed me."

"I'm sure you were very accomplished, dear," Mrs. Mishra said. "I can't do magic myself, which is why I stepped into Master Saint-Omer's line of fire. Generous Lee told me that the gun wouldn't bother me since I'm nonmagical—which I assure you isn't so bad once you get used to it. What kinds of magic could you do?"

Ali shrugged. "Oh, lots of things. Unlock doors, raise a wind," she said, waving her hands around. "That sort of thing. They usually went wrong, but still, I miss—oh!" she exclaimed as a gust of wind smacked into her and flapped her hair around her face. "Oh no!" she added as another gust of wind tore the leaves off a bush near them.

"Ali!" Sie called. "Stop that!"

"It's not me," Ali said. "It can't be, my magic's blocked. I was just telling Raahi's mother about the workings I used to do."

"It's *definitely* you," Sie exclaimed as the big red roses on a nearby bush began to explode, one after another, in puffs of petals. "Stop thinking about magic!"

"Oh! Sorry. But that's wonderful!" Ali added, smiling.

"My song-weaving undid the blocks on anyone who was listening," the platinum sorcerer said. "I hope that is helpful."

April turned to her sisters and said, "The shiny man says he fixed you! See if it's true." And then May and June began to point at nearby beds of flowers, which instantly doubled in size and became so thickly covered with gorgeous blossoms that the onlookers crowded around them, pointing and exclaiming. In their excitement, people began to pick oversized flowers to bring home—until the triplets hurried over and told them very sternly to stop.

"I hope the Hunt Club's magic wasn't restored," Raahi said. "Where are they?"

"Fear not, young man, they're back on campus receiving a stern lecture from the dean of students," the headmaster said.

"Will they be expelled?" Mrs. Mishra asked.

"In a word, it is likely, although of course there will need to be some reforming of several of them first, as they seem to be dog shaped, and we must, as a *very* reputable academic institution, have a thorough investigation followed by appropriately tailored punishments for each of them."

"*That* was a *lot* more than a word," Raahi pointed out, but he made sure to say it quietly enough that only Sie heard him.

Sie took his hand in hers and gave it a squeeze. "You're funny," she said.

"Speaking of words," Raahi whispered, "Are you good with anagrams? Because I was thinking about the name you saw on your birth cer—"

"Not now!" Sie whispered with a nervous glance at Aunt Gen, who was walking ahead of them with Raahi's mother. "Tell me about it on our way to school tomorrow."

But as they walked along, she began to think about the name on the certificate. And the harder she thought, the wider her eyes grew. "Is it possible?" she muttered. "Really?"

Raahi smiled and gave her hand a quick squeeze in return.

THE END

Until . . .

Silent Lee
and the
Mystery of the Missing
Mona Lisa

The *Mona Lisa* was stolen in 1911 and recovered in 1913. It can be viewed in that most famous of art museums, Paris's Louvre. Raahi wrote a student essay about it—but FBI agents tracked him down soon after he posted the essay on his blog. These things happen. Well, not really. At least, not to anyone but Raahi.

The FBI wanted to know what *he* had to do with the stolen painting. Because his paper had tipped them off as to who had taken it, and therefore it had been found in the home of one of the thief's descendants. *Found last night. Because of Raahi's paper!*

A new reality had replaced the old one, and in it, the painting had been missing all those years. Only Sie and Raahi remembered the old reality in which the *Mona Lisa* had been found and put back on display shortly after it was stolen.

Awkward.

And then Silent and Raahi realized that more paintings were missing. Right there in Boston, from the Museum of Fine Art. Claude Monet's famous impressionist canvases in particular. The MFA had the largest collection of Monets outside of Europe. Operative word, *had*. Now they were disappearing. Which is why the following chapter occurs in *Silent Lee and the Mona Lisa Mystery*.

Night Watch

The museum corridor was eerily quiet and lit only by the dim red light of a headlamp Silent was wearing, but it was Raahi who led the way. He did not mind the darkness, being more accustomed to using his other senses due to his limited eyesight. "Okay, here's the Monet room," he whispered. "Are there any lasers?"

"I already cut power to them," Sie said. She was strangely good at sending highly directed bolts of lightning wherever she wanted them to strike—even though storm magic was strictly forbidden.

"Okay, we're in," Raahi announced. "Now what?"

"We wait and see who tries to take the paintings," Sie said. "And catch them! Get comfortable. It might be a long night."

Little did they know that someone had slipped a sleeping draught into their water bottles. They would be found the next morning, sound asleep, in a gallery emptied of a dozen Monets worth *several billion dollars*. Which made Silent and Raahi the prime suspects in the largest art robbery in all of human history, *Mona Lisa* included.

Oops.

About the Author

As a child, Alex Hiam spent holidays in the mysterious Boston mansion of his great grandmother, where he and his twin brother explored behind secret doors where hidden stairs lead to mysterious rooms (and perhaps, if memory does not deceive, an occasional parallel world…).

A graduate of UC Berkeley and Harvard College, Hiam was awarded the English Department's Arnold Prize. But the honor he is most proud of was being entrusted as a student with the key to the iron gates of Mount Auburn Cemetery, where he would let himself in at dawn on spring mornings to watch migrating birds before the rest of Cambridge awoke. It was a strangely magical place.

He has taught at the University of Massachusetts Amherst, and he developed and taught "Making Writing Exciting!" at North Star, a learning center for self-directed teens. He has sailed the Atlantic, Gulf of Mexico, and Caribbean and plans someday to write a book about pirates. He wrote the first two Silent Lee books while living with his wife, Deirdre, daughters Sadie and Eisa, and their dog, Einstein, in an old farmhouse in Amherst, Massachusetts—along with research trips to his favorite neighborhoods in Boston. Now they live in the small town of Putney, Vermont.

For his next book, *Silent Lee and the Mona Lisa Mystery*, Alex has "cased" the galleries at the Museum of Fine Arts in Boston and met with museum staff. His interest in the painter's work was sparked many years ago by the first Monet he ever saw, which was hanging in his great grandmother's house. He remembers touching the raised brushstrokes to see how it was painted. Fortunately it's now safely beyond his reach at the Museum of Fine Arts (or is it?).

Alex was adopted from an orphanage, and he likes to weave the search for one's own backstory into his writing. Will there be further revelations about Silent Lee's mysterious parentage in his next book? Stay tuned.

You may follow Alex on Instagram @alexhiamauthor, or on the web at www.alexhiam.com, which features samples of his latest writing along with recent book reviews and his blog about how to make *your* writing exciting!

Silent Lee's
Guide to Magic

SILENT

Silent often needs to get through locked doors, so it's handy that she knows how to perform openings. Here's a basic opening: *Recludo!*

Sometimes this works better: *Refigo!*

If someone has set a protective ward on a lock, these commands will be ineffective. To remove the ward, try this: *Demolio!*

Sometimes the magic spreads beyond the lock and things begin to open that shouldn't, like the pins on the hinges. If the door begins to fall apart, shout this working as fast as you can: *Restituere integritatim!*

If you're worried that someone might use magic to break your lock, set a ward with these three commands to produce layered protection: *Protego, subduco, contego!*

To occlude something and temporarily hide it from view: *Tego!*

To perform a wind-working that blows a strong gust of air (i.e., to blow a door down if you can't get the lock to open): *Scopos ventis!*

If that doesn't produce enough wind, try an amplification: *Augere!*

While mental influences are strictly forbidden, sometimes Silent finds it necessary to employ one. For example, muddling an enemy's thoughts may give you enough time to slip away from them. Here's an influence that confuses your enemies: *Oblivisor!* (It's what Raahi used to escape the bullies from the Hunt Club.)

RAAHI

If you're worried that someone might reveal a dangerous secret, try this long-lasting influence that stops them from talking about it: *Amen dico ne quis!*

Weather-workings are forbidden, but sometimes Silent and Raahi use lightning to disable a security camera with this command: *Percutiamus fulgur!*

If it's a clear day, gather clouds before calling lightning. This command summons a storm (use with caution): *Turbine portant, veni ad me!*

Alchemy mixes ingredients to create potions, elixirs and the like. For example, a magical cup of tea for sore throats can be made from honey and warm water with mint leaves or a drop of mint syrup added. To strengthen the magic, speak this alchemical command: *Mutata in natura!*

Travel to *alienus mundos*, other worlds, is rare. A side door key to a tandem world is a key with magical programming embedded in the metal that lasts as long as the key does. It's extraordinarily difficult to create a side door, but once it's set up, anyone who has the key can get through.

If Sie's key were in danger of being taken, she might use any number of magical tricks to save it (occluding it to make it invisible, transporting it elsewhere, making it too hot to touch, etc.). She's kept her key safe so far, but there could be future attempts on it...

GEORGE'S DEPOT HACK
(which may be able to travel between worlds?)